"Will you marry me?"

She stiffened. It happened automatically.

"Good God, Christina," he said huskily, "you'd think I'd made you an indecent proposal."

She flinched at the pain in his voice. "I do love you," she said.

"Then why are you holding back?"

She wished she knew what to say. Being with Jack for the rest of her life—how could she not want it? Of course she wanted it, more than anything, yet the thought of marriage nearly choked her, made her heart go wild with uncontrollable fear. She could hardly breathe. She couldn't do it!

Ever since **Karen van der Zee** was a child growing up in Holland she wanted to do two things: write books and travel. She's been very lucky. Her American husband's work as a development economist has taken them to many exotic locations. They were married in Kenya, had their first daughter in Ghana and their second in the United States. They spent two fascinating years in Indonesia. Since then they've added a son to the family as well. They now live in Virginia, but not permanently!

Recent titles by the same author:

AN INCONVENIENT HUSBAND

MARRIAGE-SHY

BY
KAREN VAN DER ZEE

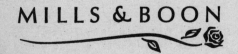

MILLS & BOON

MILLS & BOON and MILLS & BOON with the Rose Device are registered trademarks of the publisher.

First published in Great Britain 1996
Harlequin Mills & Boon Limited,
Eton House, 18-24 Paradise Road, Richmond, Surrey TW9 1SR

© Karen van der Zee 1996

ISBN 0 263 79952 2

Set in Times Roman 10 on 11¼ pt.
01-9702-54650 C1

Printed and bound in Great Britain
by Mackays of Chatham PLC, Chatham

CHAPTER ONE

THE man was a sight to behold and Christina stared at him in awe. His jeans were filthy, his boots muddy, and he had the unkempt beginnings of a dark beard. His face was rugged and tanned, and his thick black hair was too long and disheveled. He was tall, with broad shoulders, and the rolled-up sleeves of his plaid flannel shirt revealed tanned, muscular forearms.

Christina watched with trepidation as he traversed the shiny oak floor of the inn's cozy entryway-sitting room, hoping he wouldn't set foot on her precious Persian rug. He managed to avoid it by an inch, thank God.

This disreputable-looking character did not belong here in the pretty, idyllic Sleepy Hollow Inn, and she wondered why he was here, what he wanted. The guests who found their way to the inn and stayed in one of the five rooms came to spend their wedding night, or celebrate a special anniversary. Sleepy Hollow Inn was a love nest, tucked away in a small green valley in the Pennsylvania hills.

This man did not look as if he had love on his mind, or even just no-nonsense he-man sex. For one thing, he was alone. Which was not a surprise, needless to say. Not a woman Christina knew, or had ever known, would want to share a bed with him, no matter how pretty the sheets and lovely the room.

He looked like a man who hadn't made contact with water and soap for some time and was in serious need of a bath and some grooming. What he needed was to have the garden hose put on him to start with, she thought with a flash of humor, the way her mother had done to her and her sister, Anne Marie, when they'd been playing with frogs and turtles at the edge of a muddy stream or pond. This man, however, probably had not been playing with frogs and turtles. He probably lived with them in some swamp.

Dark eyes met hers and she felt an odd shiver go up and down her spine. The angles of his face were hard and strong and his nose seemed a bit crooked. The black bristle that covered his jaw gave him a distinctly sinister look. He reminded her of someone she'd seen in a movie not long ago—a villain without a conscience who robbed little old ladies.

Little old ladies. *She* was little. She was old. Oh, God. Well, not *that* old, she reminded herself, even though she had a daughter of twenty-one. Forty-two was not so old. Granted, she had some gray hair, craftily hidden with a little chemical assistance, and her belly was not as flat as it had once been and her breasts had seen perkier days, but she did still have all her own teeth and she jogged three miles every morning while the lovebirds slept in bliss in their pretty rooms, or maybe didn't sleep—who would want to know, really?

She might own a love nest, but that did not mean she spent her time thinking about love and sex. If the truth were known, she'd tried valiantly for many years now not to think of love and sex. It made life easier.

The man put his filthy hands at the edge of the antique desk she used for check-in and check-out procedures. "Great place you have here," he said, his voice deep and a bit gravelly.

"Thank you. May I help you?" Maybe he was lost and needed directions. Boy, could she give him directions.

"I'd like a room for the night if you have one available," he said, and smiled.

Her heart began to beat a little faster. She could say she was full, of course, but it would be a lie, and she didn't like to lie. Her mother had brought her up well.

The truth was that she still had the Snuggery, a small attic room with a slanting ceiling and a tiny balcony overlooking the flower garden, now ablaze with fall-blooming chrysanthemums and asters. The image of this big, dirty man moving into a romantic little room called the Snuggery was not to be dwelled on.

She could not afford to keep her rooms empty if there was a choice, but did the man have any idea of the cost of accommodation at the inn? Could he not see that this was a place of luxury and indulgence? More importantly, would he be able to pay?

"We do have one room left tonight," she said in as businesslike a tone as she could muster. "It's very small, though."

"No problem."

She took out a listing of the rates for rooms and meals and slid it toward him. "These are our rates," she stated, half-hoping it would scare him off. She would give him directions to the roadside motel seven miles down the road at the edge of town, where a room came at a fifth of the price and meals could be found in a hamburger joint next door. Surely he'd feel more comfortable there?

He barely glanced at the listing. "That'll be fine."

She gave him a registry form and watched as he wrote down his name in big, bold letters. His hand was strong and rough, the hand of a workman.

Jack Millard was his name, she noted. Method of payment: MasterCard. He reached for the back pocket of his muddy jeans, frowned for an instant, then looked back at her. "Just a moment, please. My card's in the truck."

She watched him march out the door, seeing the confident movements of his body, the broad back, the long legs. Not a bad body, actually.

She groaned at herself. An unwashed body. Good God, could she submit her other guests to the company of this unsavory character? Maybe he wouldn't want dinner and stay in his room. Then again, he looked like a man who needed food to energize that well-built frame of his. Well, maybe if he had a bath and shaved, he'd look better. Maybe not. Maybe the other guests would demand their money back and she'd go bankrupt.

Then again, her other guests probably wouldn't even notice him. Wrapped up in clouds of romance, most of them were way too preoccupied with their hormones and their partners to pay attention to anyone else.

He came back a moment later, again sidestepping the rug, and approached the desk. He had a small plastic sandwich bag in his hand, filled with what looked to be the stuff a normal person would carry around in a wallet. He fished around and found the needed credit card. A gold one, no less.

She took it from him. Jack Millard, it said. She had a sudden, frightening thought. It was a stolen credit card. In fact, that's why he was carrying it around in a plastic bag. He'd robbed somebody, emptied the wallet and tossed it, keeping only what was of use to him. Just last week she'd breathlessly watched a TV special on credit card fraud and it had been terrifying.

She would never get her money. She almost broke out in a cold sweat. She'd coddle and cosset this man in her inn to the tune of hundreds of dollars and never get paid.

She automatically went through the motions of checking him in, trying not to panic. "Will you be having dinner with us tonight?" she asked, thinking of the rabbit pieces that had been marinating in cognac since yesterday. There was enough. At well after five it was late to add another guest, but today she could probably manage it. For seventy bucks she'd give it a good try.

"Yes, I will," he said, and signed the form with a flourish.

She wondered if he'd ever paid seventy dollars for a meal before, then reminded herself that he might not do so this time if he used a stolen credit card.

"We serve a seven-course dinner starting at eight," she informed him. "In the dining room to your left."

One dark brow rose in surprise. "*Seven* courses?"

She nodded. "It's part of what makes us special. By the way, are you allergic to any food?"

He shook his head. "Not that I've discovered yet." He ran his dirty hands through his hair. "I wonder if I could have a beer."

"Certainly. Would you like it brought up to your room?"

"Thank you, yes."

She gave him a list of choices, which included very impressive beers hailing from foreign climes where they knew how to make beer. He chose a domestic one. The one construction workers went for. Why was she surprised? Not that there was anything *wrong* with being a construction worker, of course. She wasn't a snob after all. Her own very clean grandfather, whom she'd loved dearly, had been a construction worker and he'd lost two fingers building a church, a house of God. It didn't seem fair somehow.

"And could you possibly make me a sandwich to hold me over till eight?"

She nodded. "Yes, certainly." She swallowed. "Your room is at the back of the building, up the outside stairs. It's right under the roof. The name is on the door. It's the Snuggery."

"The *what*?"

"The Snuggery. It's our smallest room and very cozy."

"I see." He grinned. "Well, here I go, off to the Snuggery."

And off he went. Again she watched him. Again she noticed his strong, muscular build and the way his faded jeans fitted his body. For an instant, she even visualized him without his clothes on, and she forgot to breathe.

Something was seriously wrong with her. Thinking of men without their clothes on was not something she allowed herself to do. It was disgusting. She should be ashamed of herself. She groaned and covered her face. Since when was she thinking like a Victorian virgin?

No doubt her sister, Anne Marie, would hail the event as a sign of recovering mental health. Anne Marie was worried about her and had made it clear that what Christina ought to do was find a man and get married again or at least have a rollicking love affair.

Both ideas had been equally distasteful, which was Peter's fault. She'd been married to him for sixteen years and he'd seen to it that all her rose-colored dreams about marriage, love and sex had been squashed like bugs. Having accomplished this, he'd taken up with his secretary, a sexy young thing with perky breasts, who was twelve years younger than Christina.

She had cried, of course. Days and nights, endless nights. But here she was, a survivor, divorced now for almost six years, with her own inn full of lovebirds and no man in her own bed. It was okay. She was old now anyway. Forty-two. Nobody would want a forty-two-year-old woman with stretch marks and graying hair even if she did have all her own teeth.

"*Mother*!" her daughter, Dana, had yelled at her not long ago when she'd expressed these sentiments. "*Mom*, you're not *old*! You could be a *Playboy* centerfold with a little airbrushing! What is the *matter* with you?"

Her daughter, Dana, what a trooper. She loved the kid.

"You'd better believe," Dana had gone on, "that I'm not ever going to allow myself to dry up sexually like you're doing."

On second thought, maybe she didn't love the kid.

"I intend," Dana declared, "to have sex every day of my life until I die."

Oh, the enthusiasm of youth, not to speak of hormones. Christina got up from her chair behind the antique desk. Mr. Millard needed a beer and a sandwich. She'd tell Dana to do it. She was home from college for a long weekend and had offered to help out. But Dana was not to be found.

She went into the kitchen and found some crusty, he-man bread and made a couple of open-faced sandwiches with smoked salmon, wondering why she was bothering. The man would probably prefer some greasy lunch meat, but then, she didn't have any in her kitchen, of course, so smoked salmon would have to do.

Then the phone rang, and it was Anne Marie calling from California, in tears because her thirteen-year-old son was making her life a living hell and something was wrong with him and he'd been kicked off the school bus and now she had to drive him to school every day and she was going to kill him and so on and so forth.

By the time Christina walked up the outside stairs to the Snuggery under the roof, it was at least twenty minutes since the man had ordered his beer and sandwich. She knocked on the door and he called out for her to come in.

A cloud of warm, rose-scented air greeted her as she stepped inside the room. Obviously he had not been patiently waiting for her—she saw him through the half-open bathroom door, lounging in the tub with bubbles up to the middle of his hairy chest. He must have poured the entire bottle of bath and shower gel into the water by the looks of it.

Looking away decorously, she began to set the tray on the small coffee table.

"This probably goes against acceptable etiquette," he said, "but would you mind terribly giving it to me here? I'm not done soaking yet."

He probably wouldn't be for another month, she thought, taking in a fortifying breath and moving toward the bathroom and pushing the door open all the way. She set the tray down on a stool and put it near the tub's edge.

"Thank you." He reached for the beer and took a long gulp as if he were parched, then lowered the glass. "What is your name, if you don't mind me asking?'

Mrs. Kenley, she was tempted to say, but for some unfathomable reason, it suddenly sounded like the name of somebody very old and dried up. "Christina," she said, straightening and tucking in her stomach.

He nodded his approval. "Christina. I like that. Old-fashioned, but not stuffy." His eyes met hers, and once again that odd shiver raced up and down her spine. There was something in those eyes—a knowing, a golden glint of humor.

Intelligence.

His mouth was strong but sensuous, and the left corner tilted upward just a little. She took a step backward toward the door. "I'm glad you think it's not stuffy," she heard herself say, wanting to run.

"It's a romantic name. And you must be a romantic person working in a lovely place like this."

Only the faintest note of humor in his voice. He sensed she was nervous, idiot that she was. She should have been out of his room minutes ago, and here she was, still lingering in the bathroom doorway, while he was naked in the tub—he, a guest.

"Sit down," he went on, waving a bubbly hand toward the rose-colored toilet. "I'd like some company."

Her heart leaped in her chest. "People bring their own partners when they come here."

"Yes, I understand that," he said patiently. "Unfortunately, I am partnerless. How about you, Christina?"

"I think this is getting a little too personal, isn't it, Mr. Millard?"

One dark brow arched upward. "How much more personal can you get? You *are* here with me in the bathroom while I'm in the tub au naturel."

"And I should be in the kitchen cooking your dinner. I will see you at eight." And out she went, trying to look dignified, at which she was sure she failed miserably.

Her heart was racing as she rushed down the wooden steps and her legs were quite unsteady. She almost tripped, grabbing the railing just in time. A broken leg was not what she needed right now. Or maybe it was exactly what she needed right now. It would keep her incapacitated in her own cabin behind the inn, and she wouldn't have to face this Jack Millard at dinner tonight.

She was not stupid. It was quite clear that the man saw right through her. That he knew he made her nervous. That he realized she wondered what the hell he was doing at the inn, filthy and alone. And she was smart enough to know that this man wasn't what he looked like. His choice of words, his manner of expression, all gave him away as someone who'd not lingered in the swamps with the frogs for all his life.

She took a deep breath of the leaf-scented autumn air and tried to compose herself before entering the kitchen. Her assistant cook, all dressed up in pristine white, was busily chopping up shallots. Carl was a retired tax accountant who'd been a closet gourmet cook all his life, yearning in his soul to be a professional chef. Now he was one. And a very good one, too. As Christina spoke to him about adding one more guest for dinner, Dana sauntered in, her long blond hair neatly arranged in a

French braid. She'd shed the jeans and college sweat-shirt she'd worn earlier for black dress pants and a white silk blouse. Slim and lovely, she bloomed with the blush of youth. Her skin glowed, her hair gleamed, her big eyes shone a bright blue.

"Where were you?" Christina snapped. "I was looking for you."

At her angry tone, Dana's eyes widened in surprise. "I was in my room studying for my archaeology test. You told me to help at six."

It was 5:53. Christina felt instant remorse. "I'm sorry. I didn't mean to snap at you."

"What's wrong, Mom? Why were you looking for me?"

Christina touched Dana's shoulder. "Nothing's wrong. We had another guest arrive an hour ago. He wanted a sandwich and I got a little hassled."

Dana frowned. The idea that her mother felt hassled over a sandwich while regularly producing imaginative seven-course gourmet meals obviously was not one that went down easily.

"A man by himself?" she asked, mercifully not pursuing the issue of the sandwich hassle.

"Yes, and he's having dinner, so you'll need to set all five tables instead of just four."

"Okay, I'll get going."

At seven, she found him wandering through the sitting room, looking at a grouping of carved wooden elephants in different sizes and colors. Anne Marie had collected them while they'd lived in Tanzania as children. Their globe-trotting family had resided in a number of foreign climes and the inn's decorations included an eclectic assortment of artwork and crafts hailing from faraway places. The guests were encouraged to look around and enjoy the paintings, the wall hangings and the collection of antique dolls, African masks, colorful crystals and carved wooden Buddhas. The rooms were cozy and comfortable and invited lingering.

Jack Millard's long black hair curled damply around his ears and the dark bristle still adorned the lower part of his face. However, he wore a clean pair of Dockers and a light sweater, which was a big improvement, she had to admit.

He studied everything with great care and it made her nervous. Maybe he wanted to swipe some of it. One of her mother's antique dolls, the painting of the Indian princess. What was she thinking?

Next time she passed by the door two minutes later, he was studying the books that crowded the shelves on the walls. He took one out, opened it and leafed through it, then suddenly turned as if he had noticed her regard. She almost flushed guiltily, but not quite. Dark eyes probed hers. Deep brown with golden flecks, she noticed.

"Do you mind if I look?" he asked politely.

"No, no, of course not. That's what it's all there for."

"Fascinating," he said.

She fled back into the kitchen, where Dana was inspecting wineglasses for water spots.

"Mom! That guy! He's *gorgeous*!" she said breathlessly.

"What guy?" Christina asked. "There's five of them here."

Dana glowered at her. "You know which one."

"You mean the one with the long hair and beard stubble?"

"It looks *cool*!" Dana said emphatically. "And that *body*! Did you see it?"

"Not really, no," Christina replied, thinking of him naked in the tub, covered only with rose-scented bubbles.

Dana sighed regretfully. "He's really a bit too old for me, but he's sure good-looking." She held up a glass to the light and studied it. "He's about right for you, I'd say."

"No, thank you." Christina examined the bowl of wild mushrooms that would go into the cognac sauce for the rabbit.

"I'd consider making a move, Mom," Dana suggested, polishing a glass. "Think about it. How many single men come walking in here ever? Not a one, I believe. It's a sign, an omen."

"Who says he's single? He could be married with seven children and having an affair on the side."

"If that were the case, then he'd have wife or lover with him here, wouldn't you think? No, I'm sure it's a sign. It has to be."

"A sign of what?"

"Everything happens for a reason. There are no coincidences. He's here because you're meant to connect with him."

Christina groaned. "Where do you get that stuff?'

"It's everywhere, Mom. You just have to become aware of what's going on around you. Nothing happens without a reason."

"The reason the man is here is that he needed a place to sleep and a meal to eat, not because he should have an affair with me. Now, do me a favor and stop trying to match me up, kiddo. I'm in charge of my own love life, thank you."

"What love life?" Dana muttered, picking up the silver tray laden with spotless wineglasses.

Christina pretended not to have heard and busied herself with the preparation of the plates for the appetizer course.

Christina wished she'd had the courage to send him away when she'd had the chance. All night as she served the various courses to her guests in the small dining room, she could feel Jack Millard's dark eyes on her. His glances weren't lascivious, she had to give him that, but surreptitious and discreet. However, not discreet enough for her not to notice. She was acutely aware of his regard and it made her heart race and her hands shake. Shaking hands were a serious handicap when you were serving plates of expensive food.

He kept watching her. And he tried to talk to her, as well, while she served him his food, but she remained politely aloof, retreating as soon as possible every time.

She could not remember the last time a man had paid so much attention to her and she couldn't imagine why Jack Millard was observing her with so much interest. Something was not kosher about this man and it was not a reassuring thought, really. The man had a screw loose somewhere, no doubt.

He enjoyed the meal and took his time eating it, but in between courses she could see him reading a paperback book—an international spy thriller from the look of the cover. It was outrageous. She felt insulted, only she wasn't sure exactly why. He had no one to talk to after all, and she always left plenty of time between each course. Seven courses was a lot of food and people had to find room for all of it.

She lay in bed later that night, aware her body was tense and shivery, as if she'd overdosed on coffee. She couldn't help thinking about Jack Millard. She couldn't help seeing those dark eyes following her as she moved around the dining room—following her still, it seemed.

She couldn't sleep. Turning on the light, she picked up her favorite magazine, *Travel and Leisure*, and leafed through it.

One day she would be free to travel, to live in some exotic place and experience another kind of life—one more adventurous, more exciting. Her longings were colored by the happy memories of her childhood overseas.

She felt instantly guilty. There was nothing wrong with her life. She loved the inn; she loved the creativity of cooking wonderful food. She was her own boss and she was standing on her own two feet.

"What else can you possibly want?" she muttered to herself.

Excitement, adventure, love, said a secret little voice inside her. She groaned and pushed her face into the pillow.

Late the next morning, she noticed Jack Millard in the hammock. Everyone else had checked out and it had to be him. She crossed the leaf-littered lawn toward the two ancient trees between which the hammock was suspended. It was unseasonably warm for October, and she wished she'd worn a blouse rather than a sweater.

His eyes were closed, and for a moment she looked at his face, her heart leaping crazily in her chest. It was a strong, manly face, but as he relaxed, he looked quite peaceful and not at all threatening.

A magazine lay on the ground, dropped over the edge of the hammock, and she picked it up. *Garbage Digest* said the title on the front cover. She'd heard of the magazine, but had never seen it.

"Well, hello there," Jack said sleepily. She glanced up and saw him look at her drowsily. He wore cotton trousers and a bright red T-shirt. Red. The color of passion, the color of danger. Why was she thinking these idiotic thoughts?

She forced herself to look at him squarely. "Checkout is at noon," she said, trying to sound friendly but firm.

"What time is it now?"

"Ten minutes till twelve."

He yawned. "Oh, I'm quite comfortable here. Sign me up for another night."

She clamped her teeth together, tempted to tell him she was expecting other guests and his room would not be available, but it would be lunacy to do so. She couldn't just pass up the income, not with a business to run and a daughter in college and tuition to pay. She couldn't afford it.

"If you want to dine with us, please let us know before two," she said, caving in to economic necessity.

"I'll dine with you," he returned promptly. "Will you be working tonight?"

His question took her by surprise for a moment. "Why?"

He smiled. "If not, I wonder if I could buy you a meal, as well, and you could keep me company while I eat. This is a lovers' hideaway and sitting there all by myself last night did make me feel rather conspicuous."

He certainly hadn't looked as if he'd felt out of place. As a matter of fact, he had looked oblivious to his surroundings, watching her, enjoying the food and reading his book between courses.

"I'm working tonight," she said.

He gave her a charming smile. "And I suppose you can't tell them you're sick and then show up with me at the table."

"I also can't do it because I own the place and I'm the cook." Well, she owned half of it. Her sister, Anne Marie, owned the other half. When their parents had died in a tragic car accident four years ago, Sleepy Hollow Inn had been left to them both.

His brows shot up. "Well, my apologies for misinterpreting the situation. I should have known."

"Why should you have known? If no one told you?"

"Because you are a very classy lady and you fit very well in this environment."

Classy. Good grief. She was a classy lady with an old-fashioned, romantic name.

He made a sweeping gesture, taking in the rolling lawns, the English-style flower garden, the pond, the woods. "How big is this place?"

"Twelve acres."

He nodded thoughtfully, frowning slightly as if he was thinking of something very intently. Christina held out the magazine.

"Is this yours?"

He took it from her. "Yes. It fell and I was too lazy to get out and pick it up. So I fell asleep instead."

Somehow he did not look like a lazy man who made a habit of falling asleep in a hammock in the middle of the day. Even though she had not seen him perform any tasks that necessitated the use of major muscle groups, she sensed he was a very dynamic man with lots of energy and vitality.

And a sexual drive to match, no doubt.

Now what made her think that? She was beginning to scare herself. It was Dana's fault—Dana talking about having sex every day for the rest of her life until she died.

She turned abruptly. "I'll see you at dinnertime, then," she said automatically, squashing her annoyance with herself.

"What about lunch?" he asked.

She turned around to face him. "You didn't make reservations for lunch. There are a couple of small places in town where you can eat." The hamburger joint and a greasy-spoon diner, to be exact. "Town" was a big word for the small crossroads community. It was more what the English would call a village.

"I can't do that," he said solemnly, shaking his head.

"Why not?"

"I don't want to leave here. It will ruin everything."

"It will ruin what, Mr. Millard?"

He sighed and glanced around in a rather theatrical fashion. "It will break the spell of magic and destroy my inner serenity."

Talk about romance. The man was a veritable poet. How could she resist? She couldn't help smiling.

"We can't have that, can we? All right, I'll rustle something up for you."

She walked back to the house, feeling his eyes on her, warmer than the sun, wondering what insanity had got her in its grip.

She managed to avoid him for the rest of the day, but at dinnertime there was no choice but to serve him; serving her own food to her guests was what she always did.

He asked her how long she had run the inn, and she told him she'd started helping her parents eight years ago when they'd bought the inn as a retirement project, having spent most of their professional life overseas. After their deaths, she had taken on the job by herself.

"And what do you do for a living?" she asked casually as she poured him more wine.

"I'm a junk dealer," he said, and took a bite of the smoked-trout terrine.

"Junk dealer?" She didn't know why that should surprise her, but it did.

He nodded, his mouth full, his eyes laughing.

She stared at him, knowing she shouldn't just stand here talking to him. She should take care of her other guests, fill their glasses.

He swallowed. "Yes. You know, old stuff. I buy from people who don't want it anymore, fix it up if necessary and sell it again to people who can use it."

Maybe that's why he had shown such interest in her antiques and decorations. "You mean antiques? Furniture and that sort of thing?"

"No, not antiques. Not furniture. This trout is wonderful. You suppose I could have a second helping?"

"I...yes, of course. In a moment. I need to finish
pouring wine first."

Not antiques, not furniture. Then what? She did not
get another chance to ask as he seemed to be much more
interested in talking about her than he was in talking
about himself.

It wasn't until the meal was over and she was back in
her own room that she realized he knew a lot more about
her than she did about him. Except that he was a junk
dealer with a gold credit card he carried around in a
little plastic bag.

He left the next morning in his filthy pickup truck,
and she sighed a sigh of relief.

Two hours later, the police arrived.

Two men in uniform strode up the path to the front
door. She felt her heart rate quicken in trepidation as
she watched them come through the open doors into the
sitting area. She got up from the desk to meet them.

"May I help you?" she asked.

They showed their badges, introduced themselves and
asked politely if she could spare a few moments to answer
a couple of questions.

"Yes, yes, of course. What is it about?"

One of the officers took a careful glance around, not
answering her question. "You run quite an, uh, ex-
clusive establishment, don't you?"

She stared at him, feeling her hackles rise. Was he
wondering if she were secretly running a high-class
brothel? Or a cover for illegal drug smuggling?

"I'm not sure what you mean," she said icily.

Her tone apparently caused surprise. Then the older
man grinned. "Don't take me wrong, Mrs. Kenley. I
mean, your inn has the reputation of being a very ex-

clusive country hotel and I'm not suggesting that it is anything else.''

''Thank you, Officer.''

''May I assume that your guests are generally the kind of people who have acquired a certain level of financial comfort?''

''Yes, you may. And would you offer me the courtesy of telling me what this is about?''

''We'd like to know if you've seen anyone suspicious here in the past few days. We're looking for a man in his early to mid-forties, about six foot two, dark hair and eyes, and a beard.''

CHAPTER TWO

CHRISTINA felt the blood drain from her face. Her knees trembled violently, and for a terrifying moment, she thought she was going to crumble into an undignified heap at the feet of the two officers of the law.

She sat down instead.

The two officers glanced at each other meaningfully.

"Are you all right, Mrs. Kenley?" one of the men asked with a concerned frown.

She filled her lungs with oxygen. "Yes, I am, thank you," she managed in a voice that was not quite steady.

"Is he here now?" the other officer inquired.

"Who?" she asked. After all, she hadn't said she'd seen anybody, had she?

Her mind was in turmoil. Jack Millard was a criminal hunted by the police. She'd known it in her gut from the beginning. She'd seen it just by looking at him. She should never have let him into her precious inn. Her reputation was ruined. They would catch him and the reporters would come and it would be all over the papers that she had given comfort and aid to a criminal. She'd fed him smoked-trout terrine and rabbit in cognac sauce.

"Mrs. Kenley," the older officer asked patiently, "did someone suspicious come to your inn?"

She swallowed and closed her eyes. She saw Jack's face, the devilish gleam in his eyes, the soap bubbles in his chest hair. It made her feel warm all over. It was awful. The first man who'd made her aware of her femininity in years and he had to be a criminal. A mass murderer, a rapist, a bank robber. Oh, God, she needed help.

"Yes," she said, "I—think so."

And then, like the good citizen she was, she blurted out the sorry tale to the two rapt officers, telling them about Jack Millard's filthy clothes, his long hair, his unshaven chin and the credit card in the plastic sandwich bag.

After which, of course, she had to show them her guest log and they took down the credit card number and his name and address, which was a fake one, no doubt. After which, they thanked her for her help and departed, leaving her alone, sagging in her chair like a sack of potatoes.

At four o'clock that afternoon, the phone rang.

"Christina?"

Her breath caught in her throat. She knew that deep voice. "Yes," she said. Oh, God, why was he calling her?

"You sent the cops after me." His voice was low and slow. A meaningful pause followed his words. "Not very nice, Christina," he drawled.

She froze, her heart slamming against her ribs. Then she dropped the receiver back on its cradle as if it had burned her.

Moments later, the phone rang again. She stared at it in horror, unable to move. She'd made a terrible mistake. She shouldn't have let him stay at the inn. She should have lied to the police. Look what honesty was getting her: She was going to be stalked and terrorized by a criminal.

After the fourth ringing, it stopped. Someone had picked up the phone somewhere else in the house. Maybe Carl in the kitchen.

A moment later, Janice, who was in charge of housekeeping, came into the lobby. She looked perfect for the job, with a prim and proper face and a neat and tidy body. Not a curly gray hair out of place. "I have a message for you," she said. She stared at Christina with a frown. "What's wrong? What's going on?"

Christina swallowed and tried to get her breathing back under control. "I don't know. What's the message?"

"A man called. Jack, he said his name was. He wants you to know he did not intend to frighten you and that he's not...not in jail."

And that was supposed to make her feel better? She had visions of his coming back, creeping around the outside of her private little cabin, hiding in the bushes, trying to sneak through her bedroom window and do her serious bodily harm.

It did not bear contemplating. She really ought to stop watching scary movies.

She wouldn't need to anymore—she might just be living one.

Janice handed her a slip of paper, her face disapproving. "He left his number. He'd like you to call him at your convenience."

When hell freezes over, Christina thought wildly. "Thank you, Janice," she said, hoping she sounded normal.

Janice left and Christina glanced at the paper. It was a Philadelphia number. She checked the guest log, seeing it was not the same number as the one Jack had entered there. Maybe she should call the cops; they'd left a card in case she had anything further to report. She now had another number, which would constitute new information.

Jack was not in jail. What did that mean? That he'd escaped the clutches of the law? That he hadn't done anything? That all of this was just a colossal joke?

Some joke. She could call the number and talk to Jack and see what she could find out.

She was *not* going to call him.

She left her desk and went into the kitchen to get started on the cooking. Today, three couples were dining in and staying the night. All older. One was celebrating a forty-year anniversary. They even looked happy. And physically in good shape, too, for their age. Amazing. How did they do it?

She sighed as she glanced at the menu. Good loving is what did it, of course. Being friends. Respecting each other. Caring for each other. And if Dana were here, she'd probably say it was sex every day that would do it.

She groaned inwardly. None of these had worked well in her own marriage, and even now, after all these years, she still felt a painful regret for having failed, for not having had what she really wanted and needed. Still had a secret longing to have love and give it in return.

Grow up, she told herself. Forget it. Pay attention to the pesto.

So she paid attention to the pesto, gritting her teeth, and then Dana came in, looking gorgeous in a long, flowing skirt and a black silk blouse, her blond hair on top of her head in a loose, sexy way that only someone young could carry off.

"You look great," Christina said, smiling.

Dana grinned and swirled around. "Pretty good for only fifty bucks, isn't it?"

"Yes." Dana had style and pizzazz and a gift for finding bargains.

Dana stopped in front of her and considered Christina's outfit. "You know, Mom, we need to do something to fluff you up a bit."

Christina laughed. She couldn't help it. "Fluff me up? What kind of expression is that?"

"My very own. You know, Mom, you really look good, and you have good taste and your clothes have class, but—" Dana stopped and frowned. "I don't know, something is missing."

"Missing? Like what?"

"Life."

"*Life*? What do you mean? I look dead?"

Dana chuckled. "Not dead, no. But you need a little, er, you know, *cayenne pepper* to liven things up."

Christina laughed.

"More...zip. More...*vibrancy*." Dana grinned triumphantly. "That's it! Vibrancy! That's the word!"

Dana herself certainly did not lack vibrancy, and Christina couldn't help but smile at her. And suddenly, out of nowhere, came the odd desire for just that: zip, vibrancy, a little excitement.

"All right," she heard herself say, "how should I go about that, in your opinion?"

So they discussed fluffing her up and made a plan to go shopping in Philadelphia. Christina looked at her pretty daughter, feeling a sudden wave of warm maternal love. How lucky she was to have a daughter like Dana, to have a relationship with her that included love and trust and laughter. How many mothers got along with their daughters as well as she did?

She might not have made a success of her marriage, but as far as her daughter was concerned, she'd sure done something right.

The next morning, Tuesday, a florist's van drove up to the inn and delivered an enormous flower arrangement. Christina stared at it in amazement. It was the biggest one she had ever seen and it consisted of exotic tropical flowers that must have cost a fortune. She took out the little card and read it.

I truly did not mean to frighten you. Rest assured the police are not after me. Please accept my apologies.
                                        Jack Millard

She put the flowers in the sitting room, where they looked spectacular. No sense in throwing them away in outrage; she had earned them fair and square.

The police were not after him, his note said. He could be lying, of course. The flowers could have been purchased with the stolen credit card. She tore the enclosure up and threw it out. She didn't want Dana, or anyone else for that matter, to see it.

She was a wreck. She needed to know what was going on. So she called the number the officers had given her and told the one who answered about the scary phone call, after which he reprimanded her for not having reported it to him the instant it had happened, but fortunately, there was really nothing to worry about because Mr. Jack Millard was a respectable citizen and not the man they were after. Mr. Millard, however, had given them valuable information about the man they were actually looking for.

After she hung up, she wasn't sure if she felt reassured or not. Jack could be a con man who'd craftily sent the police on a wild-goose chase looking for somebody else who did not exist.

Stop it! Stop it! she told herself. Her imagination was working overtime. She went back to work, planning menus, forcing herself to concentrate on food rather than Jack Millard.

However, it was difficult not to concentrate on Jack Millard when an hour later she looked up and found him standing right in front of her.

She stared at him in shocked wonder. He looked absolutely magnificent. Gone were the beard stubble and the long hair. His clean-shaven chin was square and strong and his hair was fashionably short, if still thick and slightly curly. He wore sharply creased trousers of exquisite make and fit and a silk shirt patterned in various shades of heather, teal and indigo blue. A faint scent wafted across the desk—clean and manly. Her heart raced. She couldn't do a thing about it.

Her mind was a whirlwind of confusing emotions. Fear, surprise, amazement and something else she wasn't ready to analyze yet.

"Hello, Christina," he said in that deep, sexy voice of his.

She gulped. "What are you doing here?" It did not sound welcoming.

"I came to see you and apologize in person." He glanced toward the table where the flowers gloried in all their tropical splendor. "I see you got the flowers."

"Yes," she said, fighting her good manners and refusing to offer him the thank-you-they-are-so-beautiful routine.

He put his very clean hands on the edge of the desk and leaned slightly forward. "You are angry," he stated calmly.

She gritted her teeth and glared at him.

"Very angry," he amended. "Furious, in fact."

"Yes," she said hotly. "I don't know who you are, Mr. Millard, but what the hell possessed you to give me that phone call and scare the living daylights out of me?" Her voice trembled. "I hardly slept all night! I thought you might come back and murder me in my bed!"

The smile faded from his eyes and he suddenly looked a little pale, but maybe she was imagining it.

"I am truly very sorry," he said, repentance in his voice. "What possessed me was a sense of humor and a very unfortunate and ill-timed impulse to tease you."

"*Tease* me?"

He nodded. "I thought it was really quite amusing that you sent the police after me, meaning you obviously thought I was a shifty character and—"

"You *were* a shifty character! I mean, you looked like one!"

"Because I was dirty and hadn't shaved in a few days?"

"Yes, exactly."

"Isn't that jumping to conclusions?"

"I'm not going to have a debate over my thoughts and impressions, Mr. Millard," she said coldly.

"When I called you, I never thought you would take it the way you did, but the instant you slammed the phone down, it was clear what had happened. It was obvious to me then that I had made a very serious mistake, because after all you didn't know me very well. As a matter of fact, you didn't really know me at all."

"And I think I would just as soon keep it that way," she retorted.

"Does that mean you won't accept my apologies? I came all the way from Philadelphia to make them in person and you're not convinced of my sincerity?" He looked faintly wounded.

"I accept your apologies, but that doesn't mean we now have to be buddy-buddy, does it, Mr. Millard?"

A spark of humor danced in his eyes. "No. But the thought has a certain appeal."

"Well, forget it," she snapped. "Now, if you'll excuse me, I have work to do."

He inclined his head. "Of course."

She watched him leave. He looked so good. He got into a shiny cobalt blue sports car, closed the door, started the engine and zipped out of sight.

"Good riddance," she muttered.

"Mom! Did you see him?" Dana came walking across the lawn, hips swinging, a stack of books clutched to her chest.

It was afternoon and Christina was sitting on the secluded little terrace of her cabin taking a well-deserved tea break before going to the inn kitchen to start dinner. It was a glorious day, warm enough to be outside, and she was thoroughly enjoying the splendor of the trees displaying their vibrant fall colors.

"Did I see who?" she asked as Dana stepped onto the terrace.

"Jack. Jack Millard."

"I saw him this morning, yes. He left, though."

Dana dropped the books on the wooden bench and slouched into a chair. "Well, he's back. He's staying for the night, he said. We talked for over an hour. He's really nice, Mom!"

"I didn't know he had a reservation," Christina said, feeling anger rise in her.

Dana shrugged casually. "Maybe somebody else took care of it. Ah, tea. Great. What kind is it?"

"Earl Grey," Christina said automatically. "Where is he now?"

Dana waved in the direction of the pond. "Over there somewhere. I was sitting under the tree studying, when he walked by and said hi and then we just talked, that's all. He knows a little about archaeology. He was once in charge of shipping all kinds of precious artifacts from a dig in Turkey to England. His family owns the Millard Import and Export Company and I think he's filthy rich, but he didn't say that, but I can tell. He's been all over the world. Oh, and he's a widower and he has two kids, a boy sixteen and a girl fourteen."

"Well, thank you for the information, sweetheart," Christina said dryly. "He told me he was a junk dealer."

"A what?"

"A junk dealer. He was reading *Garbage Digest*."

Dana's face was something to behold. "I wonder what that is all about. I'll have to ask him." She came to her feet. "I'll get a cup and be right back."

Christina closed her eyes. Jack Millard was staying the night. Again. Something shivered through her veins. Anger, or just the teeniest bit of excitement? She clenched her jaw. Get a grip on yourself, she said silently.

Dana sat down again and poured herself a cup of tea from the big pot. "He cut his hair and shaved. I kind of like that roguish look on him, but I imagine you think he looks better now."

"I didn't think about it," Christina lied.

Dana glowered at her. "Don't lie," she said. "Of course you thought about it. You *saw* him, didn't you? And you're not *dead*, are you? The man is sexy like crazy. Don't you tell me you didn't notice!"

Being close to your daughter was wonderful. Most of the time. This was not one of those times.

"Dana," Christina said, trying to sound patient, "I know what you are thinking. But believe me, I'm not interested. I don't *need* a man."

Dana studied her over the rim of her cup. "Mom, I know you don't need one to keep you, to financially take care of you, but don't you *want* one?"

Christina shook her head. "No, Dana, I don't want one," she said calmly. She'd had a man once and that was enough.

Dana bit her lip, her blue eyes distressed. "It's Dad's fault," she said. "He did this to you. He made you think that all men are like him. Well, they're not, Mom!"

Christina sighed. "I know that, sweetheart. Honestly. I'm not cursing all the males of the species because I had a bad experience with one. Give me some credit, all right? It's just . . . I'm happy with the way my life is right now." She loved her independence, the peacefulness of her life. She loved not having to answer to anyone and not having to please anyone on a personal level.

Dana looked pained. "But you're alone all the time, Mom. I worry about you! I just wish you'd find someone special, you know. Some really great guy who's totally crazy about you."

Christina laughed. "Oh, Dana. You're young, and that's what you want for yourself, but I'm okay the way I am. Really."

Dana stared at her. "I don't believe this, Mom. You act as if your life is over."

"Oh, it's not over. I have lots of plans."

"Like what? Bingo in Florida?"

"Dana!"

Dana rolled her eyes. "Okay, okay, I'll shut up." She rose to her feet and gathered her books. "I'd better get my stuff and hustle on back to the big bad city. My test is first thing tomorrow morning. Wish me luck."

"Why are you here?" Christina quietly asked Jack as she served him the appetizer course that night.

He was sitting at a small table in the corner of the dining room, wearing impeccable gray trousers and a light sweater—casual, but expensive-looking.

He raised a quizzical brow. "Why is anyone here? Because this is a wonderful place to be. I like the peace and quiet." He glanced down at the tiny, delicate Roquefort soufflé resting in a ruby red port sauce. "And the food is spectacular. This looks delicious."

"I hope you like it," she said, unable to think of anything else to add, and went back to the kitchen to finish preparations for the soup course.

It was a good thing Carl was so competent, because she had a hard time keeping her mind on what she was doing. Jack Millard was making her nervous and she didn't seem to be able to do anything about it.

And why was he making her nervous?

Because he was paying attention to her, that's why. Because he was looking at her with more than casual interest. Because he had come to the inn to see her—she wasn't so naive as not to realize that.

And because she couldn't deny that she was very much aware of him as a man, and had been from the moment he had stridden into the inn, dirt and all.

He made her feel things she hadn't felt for a long time, made her feel aware of herself as a woman, and it frightened her. She didn't know what to do with these feelings.

"You're pathetic," she muttered to herself as she swirled a dollop of sour cream in the soup.

"Why didn't you bring someone with you this time?" she asked him as she placed the soup plate in front of him. "You didn't just happen to pass by today."

"You mean a woman?" He looked right at her.

"Of course I mean a woman," she snapped. "You must have an endless list of candidates for a romantic interlude in the country."

He grinned. "An endless list? Now what makes you think that?"

"Don't be coy with me," she said. The man was handsome, rich, sophisticated, charming. He had to have a list a mile long with women panting after him.

He shrugged. "There's no woman in my life, at least not of the variety I would want to take for a romantic night in the countryside."

His eyes held hers and she dropped her gaze to the table, feeling an odd uneasiness.

"Enjoy your soup," she said and fled.

She worked on the pasta course, her mind going wild. Why did a man like Jack Millard have no woman in his life? Maybe he had a dark side. Maybe he played games with women, like the one had played with her, pretending he was what he wasn't. She frowned as she grated some Parmesan cheese. He was a junk dealer, he'd told her. He'd told Dana something altogether different this afternoon.

The guy was a con man. She didn't trust him. He was probably playing some other sort of game with her this very minute. He'd cased her out as a lonely, over-the-hill female with droopy breasts and no sex life and intended to have a little fun with her, just for the hell of it.

Hah!

Her gaze alighted on the jar of cayenne pepper. It was very tempting to sprinkle a liberal dose of the stuff on his pasta, which would ruin the dish for sure and do some unfortunate things to his taste buds.

Taking a deep breath, she went back to the dining room and served her guests their pasta, going to Jack's table last, feeling her unease begin to bubble into anger.

"You look angry and suspicious," he stated before she could even describe the particulars about the pasta dish she was placing in front of him.

"Why did you lie to me about being a junk dealer?" she asked in a low voice.

His brows shot up. "I didn't."

"My daughter tells me your family owns an import-export company. At least that's what you told *her*."

He nodded. "So we do."

"So what's this about being a junk dealer?"

He motioned to a chair. "Sit down, and I'll explain it to you."

She had no time, of course, and besides, she wasn't that interested.

"I have work to do," she said brusquely, and moved away.

KAREN VAN DER ZEE 37

He tried to engage her in conversation as she served him the other courses and poured his wine, but she said little, which did not seem to discourage him at all.

"You have a beautiful, charming daughter," he said as she served him his dessert. She tensed instinctively and he noticed. He met her eyes and she saw a flicker of anger. "And please take that at face value. I am forty-five years old and I do not go lusting after twenty-one-year-old college girls."

"That's a comfort," she said under her breath, aware that the guests at the other tables were uncomfortably close.

"She reminds me of my own daughter," he went on. "Nicole is only fourteen, but she has the same frankness and openness your daughter has. I like that."

It was a compliment. And she had to say something. So she said thank-you and did he want more wine?

She finished serving dessert to her other guests, then made the rounds with the coffeepot and the tray of liqueurs.

"What are you doing after dinner?" he asked as she poured his coffee. "You're not in charge of doing dishes, are you?"

"No," she said truthfully. "I'm going to bed. I'm dead." An unfortunate choice of words. "On my feet," she added as an afterthought.

"You can rest your feet sitting in a chair. Let's have a drink, you and I, and talk. I'd like to clear up a few things."

"There's nothing to clear up," she said tightly. "You are a guest. All I want is for you to pay your bill and leave me alone."

"Oh, really?" he said softly, meeting her eyes.

Her heart turned over. "Yes, really," she said coolly, standing there like a fool with the coffeepot in her hand, not moving. Why didn't she move? Why not go to the next table and pour more coffee?

It was his eyes, those mesmerizing dark eyes keeping her captive. Invisible vibrations between them. Sparks flying. She was losing it.

"Well," he said slowly, "I want something from you."

Here we go, she thought to herself.

"Another cup of coffee?" she asked sweetly.

"No. Ten minutes of your time. To clear my conscience." He offered her a charming smile. "So I can sleep soundly tonight."

And why should I care if you sleep soundly tonight, she thought nastily, surprising herself by her own cattiness.

"All right," she heard herself say. "Ten minutes, in the library."

CHAPTER THREE

As ALWAYS in the fall and winter, a fire burned in the large fieldstone fireplace. They sat in deep, comfortable chairs on either side, Jack with a snifter of Courvoisier in his hands and Christina sipping from a tiny glass of Grand Marnier. The sweetness was soothing and she felt in need of soothing. Her nerves were jittery and it annoyed her to feel this way.

None of the other guests had come to sit by the fire and the two of them were alone in the warm, intimate room with its books and artwork and softly glowing lamps.

"Now, ask away," Jack said. "Anything."

What made him think she was interested? Or did he assume that all women were automatically interested in him because he was good-looking and rich and drove that outrageous blue sports car?

"I have no questions," she said calmly. "You were the one who wanted to talk to me."

"You had a question about my being a junk dealer."

"I don't care if you are or not," she said tightly. "I just don't like being lied to."

"I didn't lie. I was just dramatizing a little for the fun of it. Don't look so serious, Christina. Smile."

She glared at him. "Listen, I've just spent the past few hours on my feet, working. I'm tired and I'm in no mood to sit here and keep you company for the *fun* of it!"

"I'm sorry about that. You look like someone who could use a little fun."

39

Anger rose to her head. Now what did he mean by that? First Dana telling her she needed some pizzazz, and now this man saying she looked like she needed some fun. What did all this add up to?

She was a middle-aged, dried up, boring woman without a sense of humor.

Oh, God, what was happening to her?

She glared at Jack—handsome, dynamic and not at all boring. "When I decide to need some fun, I'll go get it, thank you," she said coldly.

"What do you normally do when you're not working?" he asked as if he were actually interested.

What she did for entertainment was read her travel magazines and adventure books. About people trekking through the Papau New Guinea jungle, about people canoeing down the Amazon River or traversing the Sahara Desert west to east on a camel, almost dying in the process. It was all very exciting, dreaming and fantasizing about all these exotic adventures, and also very safe sitting there in her cozy little cabin surrounded by the peaceful countryside. She was not about to tell him about her fantasies for a little more drama in her life.

She took another sip of the Grand Marnier. "You wanted ten minutes to talk to me," she reminded him. "To clear your conscience."

He nodded. "Right. I want to explain why I looked the way I did two days ago."

"It's none of my business."

His smile was slow and amused. "Oh, but you thought it was. You were afraid I wouldn't be able to pay my bill. You probably thought I had a stolen credit card."

She stiffened in her chair and he laughed.

"Bingo."

He had a wonderful laugh, warm and rich, which did treacherous things to her equilibrium. "Was it that obvious?" she couldn't help asking.

"I'm afraid so. You were very polite, but your face is an open book for someone who can read."

This was not encouraging news. Her face being an open book was bad enough, but for him to be a person who could read it was disconcerting.

She tensed. "So why didn't you say something?"

"I was having fun."

"*Fun*?" He'd used the word three times in the past three minutes. Apparently he liked having fun. He was probably a totally useless, shiftless, rich person, who only lived for pleasure. It was Monday, for Pete's sake, and he was here, lazing around doing absolutely nothing.

He nodded. "It was like being somebody else. Playing a role, seeing people react to me and talk to me in a whole different way than they normally do. It was quite enlightening."

She could imagine. She took a sip from the sweet liqueur. "Why did you look as if you'd crawled out of a swamp?"

He grinned. "Because I had, more or less. I'd helped a couple of guys dig out their truck that had slipped halfway into a pond. They'd been fishing. So they said. I found them a bit suspicious, but I gave them a hand anyway. One of the guys had a beard, dark hair—"

"Don't tell me," she said, interrupting him, "that he was the guy the police were looking for?"

"Correct. He'd held up a gas station."

One of the burning logs shifted and sparks danced into the air. "I'm afraid the description the police gave me fitted you," she said, refusing to say she was sorry.

"As I found out to my considerable surprise when they arrived at my office yesterday afternoon. My secretary was quite appalled." Humor colored his voice. "It was interesting that my muddy and unkempt appearance led to the police wanting to check out if I'd held up a gas station."

"It wasn't just that," she said defensively. "You carried your credit card in a sandwich bag! And your hair looked terrible and you hadn't shaved in God knows how long, like you might have been on the run or something."

I liked that roguish look, Dana had said.

He nodded before taking another sip of his cognac. "All right, fair enough. My papers were in a plastic bag because during my heroic struggles to get that blasted truck out of the pond, I slipped and ended up sitting in the water, and my wallet was soaked."

This still didn't explain why he'd been running around in a battered pickup truck with camping gear in it, and why his hair had been practically down to his shoulders. Not that she cared. Not that it was any of her business. She looked at his smooth-shaven chin, the glimmer of humor in his eyes and knew that she was fooling herself: She did care. She was curious. She wanted to know. Something about this man was hopelessly appealing. Something about him stirred all kinds of restlessness inside her. Very disturbing.

"I'd been out wilderness camping in the mountains with my sixteen-year old son. Male-bonding sort of stuff," he went on as if he'd guessed her thoughts. "I don't always have a lot of time to spend with him during the year, so I make a point to do something special for just the two of us when I can," he added.

Christina couldn't help but be considerably impressed by this information and listened raptly as he continued. He'd taken the boy out of school to do it, he told her, saying sometimes school did not come first. Since his son's academic performance was good, it wouldn't hurt missing a week. He'd put his son on a private plane back to Philadelphia and driven the pickup back alone, which he said he enjoyed.

"So that's why you hadn't shaved, but your hair wouldn't grow down to your shoulders in a week."

His mouth quirked. "You didn't like my hair?"

She shrugged. "I noticed it, that's all. Men can do what they like with their hair. Like their clothes and their language, it's an expression of who and what they are, just as it is with women."

"So I gathered. You apparently decided that my appearance expressed a criminal personality and sent the cops after me."

"I'm not going to apologize for it, so forget that."

He inclined his head, his eyes gleaming. "The long hair and beard stubble were due to a bet with my daughter. She said I looked too stuffy and needed to lighten up a little. To her that meant growing my hair and a beard. She's fourteen."

Christina thought about Dana saying she needed to spice up her appearance, but thought it better not to mention it. She didn't want his attention on her person, considering the fact that she lacked vibrancy and sexiness and probably all kinds of other necessary things to be alive and female.

"So you did what your daughter wanted?" she asked. "Just like that?"

"She challenged me, saying I didn't have the guts to do it," he said with mock defensiveness. "What was I supposed to do? Let her think I have no guts?"

Christina laughed. She couldn't help it. "So what did she think when she saw you after you came back from your camping trip, beard and all? Did she like it?"

He gave a crooked grin. "She said I looked cool."

"Cool enough to have someone send the police after you," she said dryly.

"She thought that was cool, too."

Christina made a tortured sound, something between a laugh and a groan. "Oh, God, kids."

He sipped his brandy. "I enjoyed talking to your daughter this afternoon. She's a smart kid."

The wicked sparkle in his eyes did not escape her. Christina remembered what he had said earlier that evening, about Dana being open and frank, and she wondered what her talkative daughter might have told him.

"And she, with all her charming frankness and openness, has probably told you my whole sorry past," she said with a fatalistic sigh.

"I imagine there is a lot more than what she told me."

"What did she tell you?"

"Just some basic facts. That you've been divorced for six years and that you're the most wonderful mother in the world."

"Well, that's nice. She's the most wonderful daughter in the world." A warm glow of maternal pride spread through her.

His smile teased her. "She also said you're forty-two and acting like you're eighty and your life is over."

The glow stopped glowing. She groaned. "I'm going to kill her."

He laughed. "Kids can be so cruel," he commented, possibly to comfort her. "Do you feel like your life is over?"

"No," she snapped.

"Why does your daughter think you act like it?"

Because I'm not having sex every day of my life, she answered silently. She shrugged carelessly. "She's twenty-one. She's a college student. She goes to parties and rock concerts and archaeology digs in Mexico and is busy with five thousand things. I'm twice her age and work for a living and Philadelphia is about as far as I've been in the past few years. Of course she thinks I act as if I'm ancient."

He nodded. "My daughter thinks I'm an old fuddy-duddy because I 'never do anything' as she says, and I should be having more fun."

And is it true that you aren't having any fun? she was tempted to ask, but didn't. This conversation was getting much too personal, but there was no doubt in her mind that this man was anything but a fuddy-duddy. Perhaps to a teenager it seemed that way, but he was very obviously a dynamic, sexy man and wouldn't have any trouble finding entertainment if he wanted it.

He studied her over the rim of his glass. "I haven't told you what I do in my function as a junk dealer." He gave her a questioning smile. "Are you interested?"

"You said you were dramatizing."

He grinned. "Well, it's more a sophisticated type of recycling business. It's a sideline of the company, not yet profitable, but good for Mother Earth. We recondition discarded computers, medical equipment such as CAT scans and X-ray machines, and sell them to businesses and hospitals in Third World countries."

"Why are they being thrown out if they're still good?"

"Because the business and medical worlds in this country want the most sophisticated, state-of-the-art equipment and discard computers and machinery that are still perfectly operational. Why fill up the dumps with them when they can still be of good use to businesses and hospitals in less wealthy places?"

"If you're not making a profit, why are you doing it?"

He shrugged. "For a number of reasons. For one thing, because it's the right thing to do and the company can afford to do it, and of course it makes good PR. It's socially responsible." He gave a crooked little smile. "And because I was getting excruciatingly bored with business as usual and I stood on my head until they gave me permission to go ahead with the project. I wanted the challenge to do something different, and preferably something that made sense in the larger scheme of things."

"Some junk dealer," she said lightly, trying not to show how truly impressed she was.

He laughed. "One man's junk is another man's treasure." He put his glass down and came to his feet. "My ten minutes are long gone. You've been very generous."

She looked at her watch, amazed to see how much time had passed and feeling, unaccountably, a twinge of regret that he was leaving. She rose to her feet, as well, and looked at him, seeing a dark glint of humor in his eyes.

"I enjoyed talking to you," he said.

She nodded. "I hope now that you've confessed all your many sins, you can sleep peacefully."

"As long as you accept my apology for frightening you." He moved a little closer, his dark eyes still looking into hers with that roguish gleam in them. "I would very much like to make it up to you."

Her heart made a nervous little leap. "Apology accepted," she said. "And you sent me flowers and gave me your business by staying here." She tried to smile confidently. "Tell your friends about Sleepy Hollow Inn—we do catering, too, by the way—and we'll declare your slate wiped clean."

He made a dismissive gesture with his hand. "You can't let me off the hook so easily. I insist on doing something a bit more substantial. What I had in mind was to entertain you for an evening—theater and dinner in Philadelphia. Would that appeal to you?"

Would it appeal to her to be entertained by a rich, sexy man with dinner and a play? She, who always did the cooking and the entertaining? She, who hadn't been inside a theater for years?

"No, thank you," she said politely. "That's not at all necessary. And now I really have to go."

She wanted to run, away from this man with his dark, compelling eyes, away from the feelings he stirred inside her. If ever she wanted a man who stirred her feelings, this man wasn't the one. He was way out of her league. He could have any number of beautiful young women. What would he want with her, a divorcée in her forties with wrinkles and graying hair and menopause on the way?

"Think about it," he said mildly. "I'll see you to-morrow. Good night, Christina."

"Good night," she returned, watching his back as he left the room, surprised he didn't press her further. He didn't seem at all like a man who easily took no for an answer. Maybe he was relieved. Maybe he'd only asked her out of some misguided gentlemanly sense of duty and had hoped she wouldn't accept anyway.

She stared into the fire, feeling its warmth on her face and hands, trying not to feel the treacherous yearning welling up inside her.

She couldn't sleep. She tossed and turned, thinking about Jack, thinking about her ex-husband. Thinking about what Dana had said. *I just wish you'd find someone special, you know. Some really nice guy who's totally crazy about you.* She groaned into the pillow. The last thing she wanted was another man.

She was happy with her life, wasn't she? She loved being on her own, not having to feel the constant stress of living with someone else—like Peter, always critical, always disapproving.

Looking back, she couldn't imagine how she'd stayed in the marriage so long. He had squashed something precious inside her—her self-confidence, her joy and creativity.

And she had allowed him to, for sixteen long years.

Now she had peace. People complimented her rather than criticized her. She had her own business, and although it wasn't always easy to make ends meet, she was happy. She was free, she was independent, she felt safe.

Only something was missing in her life. Pizzazz, Dana would say. Excitement, adventure.

To her own discomfort, she had to admit that Jack's presence created that element of excitement and adventure. She craved this secretly, yet it frightened her at the same time. It had taken her so long to find this inner peace, to rebuild her sense of confidence, to realize she was not as incompetent and stupid as Peter had insinuated she was.

It had taken a long time to build up her confidence again, and the inn had been the perfect place for her efforts. It had given her an opportunity to develop her creativity in decorating and cooking, as well as her business skills in running the place.

What she hadn't developed was her skill with men. She hadn't wanted to. All she had wanted was to stay away from men, from romance, from all matters of the heart. Never again did she want to go through what she had experienced in her marriage to Peter.

She didn't want to think about Peter. It was over and she was happily free of him. She had learned her lesson well. No more men in her life. And that included Jack Millard with the devil in his eyes.

She didn't want to think about Jack, either. Impatiently, she tossed the comforter aside and got out of bed. Lying here wide awake was dangerous. She put on a comfortable terry robe and her slippers and went into the small kitchen and made herself a mug of hot cocoa.

She took it outside into the crisp autumn night—clear sky, lots of stars. The air had a clean, woodsy scent. She took in a deep breath, savoring the silence, the peacefulness.

Her eyes caught a movement in the trees, and she noticed a solitary figure sitting on the old wooden bench. She peered into the darkness, knowing somehow that it was Jack, that he was sitting there alone, looking at the moon as she was.

And she knew he had to see her, too. The living-room light was on; he had to see her silhouetted against it as she stood here on the terrace.

Jack looked at the small figure standing on the terrace of the cabin, feeling his pulse leap. Christina. Christina with the small, vulnerable face and the big blue eyes. He'd loved watching her this evening, maneuvering around the small tables in the dining room, serving her guests their meals. She moved with a natural, sensual grace that had no artifice in it. Just watching her made his pulse speed up. And she had the most beautiful mouth he had ever seen—soft, full lips that begged to be kissed and tasted.

He felt like an idiot staring at her from a distance, acting like a lovesick teenager rather than the grown man he was. Yet he couldn't stop thinking about her, couldn't even sleep because in his mind he kept seeing her face, hearing her soft singsong voice. From the moment he had entered the inn and caught the fearful suspicion in those blue eyes, he had been lost.

He was an old fool.

An old, lonely fool.

Christina watched him come to his feet and stroll down the narrow path toward her. Her heart began to flutter uneasily. She could simply go inside, lock the door, turn off the light, but she did not. She stood there, barely breathing, watching him move through the moonlight shadows, calm and unhurried, yet with clear direction.

He stopped at the edge of the terrace, politely distant. "Couldn't sleep, either?" he asked.

"No."

"It's a beautiful night."

"Yes." She shivered a little and took a sip of the steaming cocoa. "Aren't you cold?" she asked then, seeing he was only wearing a sweatshirt and no jacket.

"There's a certain nip in the air," he acknowledged.

She lifted the mug in her hand. "Would you like some hot chocolate?" she heard herself ask. Good Lord, what in the world possessed her?

"I'd love some." He sounded amused. "I can't remember the last time I had hot chocolate."

"I can add a shot of rum to it if you want to make it more sophisticated," she offered, "or Kahlúa."

He stepped onto the terrace and came toward her. "Just plain hot chocolate is fine," he said.

She turned and entered the living room. "I'll be a couple of minutes," she said over her shoulder. "You can come in if you want."

What kind of insanity caused her to invite the man into her cabin in the dead of night? A man she hardly knew at that. She was suddenly embarrassingly aware of her inelegant appearance in the unflattering bathrobe and functional slippers, her face devoid of makeup, wrinkles unobscured. She looked like a dowdy housewife who'd given up all hope. She stared blindly at her fumbling hands as she made another mug of cocoa. Too late now—the deed had been done.

She stirred the hot drink, sloshing some over the edge of the cup. Oh, who cared what she looked like? After all, she was only offering him cocoa, not a night of passion.

Returning to the living room, she found him looking through her travel magazines.

"Thank you," he said as she placed the steaming cup on the table in front of him.

She opened the doors to the wood-burning stove, picked up a poker and stirred up a fire in the smoldering ashes.

"Have you traveled much?" he asked.

"Not as an adult, but as a kid I lived in several places overseas. My father was in the Foreign Service." She put another log on the fire and turned her head to look at him. "And you?"

He nodded. "All over the globe, for the business." He glanced down at the magazine in his hand. It showed the glittering temples of Bangkok. "Looks like you're still interested."

She put the screen in front of the fire and left the doors open. "I am, but I can't do it now, for obvious reasons." She sat down in a chair and picked up her own cup.

"Tied hands and feet to the inn, I imagine."

"Yes." She didn't know why she felt defensive. "I'll travel when I retire."

"Retire?" His eyebrows shot up in surprise. "Is retirement something you actually think about?"

"Shouldn't I?" Her tone was defensive.

"Retirement won't be here for another twenty-some years. You have a life to live before that. What do you intend to do with that?"

"I intend to run the inn," she said. "Is something wrong with that?"

"Not a thing," he said calmly. "If that's what you want. You're obviously very good at it."

"And I enjoy it. I'm independent, I'm my own boss, and that counts for something even if I don't have time to do other things I want. We can't have everything in life."

He gave her a crooked grin. "Really? Don't disillusion me."

"You, of course, have everything you want in life," she said lightly.

He rolled his eyes. "I'm a single parent with two teenage kids. Life is perfect."

She laughed in spite of herself. "Tell me about your children. Are they manageable?"

"Manageable? Now there's a good word. Yes, they're manageable, thank God, which is more than can be said about me when I was their age. They're good kids, and they do well in school, and I really have little to complain about if we don't count the way they dress or their taste in music." He gave a wry smile. "Of course, it would be nice if they'd take me and my opinions seriously once in a while."

"That's a lot to ask for when they're teenagers. Just wait, and suddenly they'll realize they *don't* know everything, and that you actually may have something to offer them in terms of understanding and wisdom."

"The voice of experience." He smiled. "You have a good relationship with your daughter, don't you?"

"Yes." She finished the rest of her cocoa and put the cup down.

He studied her for a moment. "Have you ever thought of getting married again?" he asked.

"No," she said flatly.

"Why not?"

"I like my independence." I like coming home and finding peace and quiet, she added silently. I like not being criticized for everything I do.

He searched her face. "Didn't you feel you were independent while you were married?"

"No." She didn't want to talk about it. She looked away to stare at the struggling fire. "What about you?" she asked quickly. "Do you want to get married again?"

He gave a rueful smile. "I keep telling myself I've given up looking, but—" he shrugged "—I don't think I really have. I think, secretly, I want a wife again."

"Why? I mean—"

"I liked being married."

She wanted to know why he had liked it. She hesitated briefly. "Didn't it make you feel tied down?"

"Tied down like what?"

She shrugged. "Like not having the freedom to do what you wanted to do, have other women or something."

He laughed. "Other women or something?" He shook his head. "No." His eyes held hers for a long moment and the laughter was gone, replaced by a softening of his expression. "I didn't want other women," he said quietly.

She swallowed, digesting his words, feeling an odd pang of envy. Lucky woman, his wife.

"Your wife must have been special."

"Yes, she was."

She looked down at her hands, feeling his gaze on her.

"You were divorced," he said then, "so I assume you were not too happy being married."

"No, not too much," she said, forcing herself to sound light.

"How bad was it?" he asked. "Or shouldn't I ask?"

"Most people thought our marriage was perfect, actually. You know—a handsome, charming husband, a beautiful house, money, clothes, a lovely little daughter."

"So what was wrong with the perfect picture?"

"The charming husband didn't really think his wife was so perfect," she said dryly. "And guess what—he was right." His brows shot up, but before he could ask

another question, she got up from her chair and started
poking the fire again. "Are you warm enough?" she
asked.

"I'm fine."

He paused for a long moment. "So your husband expected you to be perfect. Not an easy assignment."

"But I gave it my best," she said, adding a note of
melodrama to her voice. "I tried for sixteen years and
gave up. I decided I just didn't have it in me to be
perfect." She sighed theatrically. "Boy, what a relief it
was to admit that to myself. And now that I'm no longer
married I can just be my own flawed self with abandon."

He laughed. "Ah, such joy. Tell me about all your
flaws."

"Not on your life."

He grinned. "Tell me about your charming husband,
then. What kind of man was he?"

"A very flawed one." She smiled nicely. "Was the hot
chocolate good?"

He smiled at her, holding her gaze for a long moment.
"The best I ever had. And now it's time for me to get
going. We should both try to get some sleep."

"Yes." She was relieved he wasn't hard to get rid of.

He stood up and she found herself facing him, a little
too close for comfort. He was looking at her with those
dark eyes and she felt her pulse quicken.

"What's the matter?" she asked.

He gave a crooked little smile. "I'm fighting off a
strong impulse."

"And what's that?" she asked, mentally kicking
herself as she heard herself ask the question. Was she
really so naive that she needed to ask?

"The impulse to kiss you."

Her heart lurched. "Keep fighting," she said, managing to smile back. "You look like you're the winning
type." She moved to the door and opened it.

His eyes did not leave her face as he made to leave. He stood still in front of her as the chilly night air wafted around them.

"Oh, what the hell," he muttered, leaning toward her and kissing her. Just a simple kiss, a simple brush of his warm lips across hers, and then he straightened. "Sometimes," he said softly, "I'm just a weakling. It's one of *my* many flaws. Good night, Christina."

She stood there, her heart racing like a teenager's, her legs trembling. It was pathetic.

The large and hearty breakfasts at the inn were as famous as the dinners, but Carl was in charge of them. He had the help of Susie, who did the serving and the cleanup. This gave Christina the luxury of taking it easy in the mornings, enabling her to have a good run and a light breakfast at home in the cabin before going to work. It also afforded her the opportunity to avoid Jack Millard, the man who had kissed her, the man who loved his kids and recycled junk for the good of mankind.

Unfortunately, he had not yet checked out as she had hoped he would have. She'd been at her desk in her tiny office barely ten minutes when he appeared in the open door, wearing tan slacks, a shirt and tie, and a dark blue blazer fitting perfectly over straight shoulders. Her heart turned over in her chest at the sight of all this male splendor. He looked fit and rested and ready to take on the world.

"Good morning," he said. "Breakfast was delicious."

"Thank you. I thought you'd left already."

"No hurry this morning." He smiled easily. "Have you given any thought to my dinner invitation?"

"I appreciate the gesture, but I have to decline," she said politely.

"What are you afraid of?" he asked quietly.

She fought down an angry reply. "Afraid?" she echoed, trying to sound unperturbed. "I'm not afraid of anything. I just don't see a reason for us to go out."

"Well, maybe I can help you out with a couple of reasons."

"I don't need help, thank you," she said coolly.

He gave her an assessing look. "Mmm. Maybe your daughter was right," he said slowly. "Maybe you do feel as if your life is over."

She grew hot with indignation. His eyes were gleaming and she knew he was amusing himself. She managed a tight little laugh. "Because I don't want to go out with you?"

He shrugged lightly. "Have you gone out with anyone lately?"

She clenched her teeth. No, she hadn't. She'd been too busy. Well, that was one excuse. "My personal life is none of your concern," she said sharply. "And my going out with men, or not going out with men, is not a reflection of whether I think my life is over!"

"No, it isn't," he agreed, moving a step closer. "But I find it hard to believe you're not interested in an evening out, no strings attached."

No strings attached, my foot, she thought. She already felt plenty of strings yanking at her all over the place. She pushed her chair back and stood. He was too tall and overpowering and she didn't like him looming over her.

"I simply don't want to deal with it," she said, trying to sound businesslike. "I want to keep my life simple."

He nodded. "Sounds like the I'm-over-the-hill syndrome to me."

She gasped. "What?"

"I'm sorry. I was a little too blunt." He smiled charmingly. "However, I don't think you're over the hill," he added softly, standing right in front of her now.

"I like you, Christina. I am attracted to you. What's wrong with that?"

Before she could answer, he reached out and kissed her. Not a simple stroking of his mouth over hers this time, but an honest-to-goodness sexually stimulating he-man kiss that stunned her completely, sapping all energy from her. Overpowering her senses. Evaporating all resistance. Her body yielded against his as if it were the most ordinary thing to do. And that at ten in the morning.

He stopped as abruptly as he began, leaving her reeling on her feet. She fumbled for the edge of the desk to steady herself.

He grinned at her. "There's quite a bit of life left in you, Christina. Don't waste it. And now I shall leave. If you change your mind about having dinner with me, let me know. You have my number."

And off he went, striding into the autumn sunshine toward his cobalt blue sports car.

She dragged in a deep, shuddering breath, still feeling his mouth on hers, still smelling the woodsy scent of his after-shave. Never before had she been kissed like this, not even by the man to whom she'd been married for sixteen years. She felt as if she'd been thoroughly ravished, yet all he had done was hold her and kiss her.

Leaning weakly against the desk, she closed her eyes. One thing Jack had proven to her: She wasn't dead sexually. Not by a long shot.

The knowledge should be comforting, yet all she felt was terror.

She didn't change her mind about having dinner with him. She didn't call him. Two weeks went by and she heard nothing from Jack Millard. She was relieved. She was beginning to forget him. Well, that's what she told herself.

Then one afternoon she found a message on her desk, saying that Jack Millard's secretary had called to see if she could make arrangements to have a business dinner catered at Jack Millard's private residence. A sit-down dinner for twenty. Could Christina please call back at her convenience?

Christina stared at the message in her hand, feeling a fearful sense of inevitability rise inside her. A catered dinner for twenty. It was business she couldn't possibly turn down. It would be insanity to reject it just because she didn't want to see Jack again.

Oh, God, she was scared to death to see him again.

She didn't want a disastrous affair. She didn't want to get hurt again. She wanted to protect herself from disillusion and despair.

How could she possibly not get hurt with a man like Jack? He was too handsome. He was too rich. He was too charming. He was so wrong for her.

Yet he made her every cell stand at attention. He made her blood tingle and her body shiver with his nearness. He made her feel all kinds of long-forgotten womanly yearnings. It was a nightmare.

She dropped her head on her arms and moaned.

CHAPTER FOUR

LATE that night, Christina sat in the bathtub and contemplated the situation. The water was fragrant with rosemary and juniper oil, which was supposed to soothe the nerves. She needed all the soothing she could get. A glass of wine by her side would help, too, she hoped.

Catering a dinner for twenty was a business deal pure and simple, she told herself. The fact that it was at Jack Millard's house didn't make it anything else. He liked her food and he wanted it served to his guests. Nothing personal. She grimaced. It would be nice if she could actually believe this. It would be nice if she didn't need the money.

Everything happens for a reason, Dana had said. There are no coincidences. So what was the reason for this? Probably to test her strength in the face of temptation. A man like Jack Millard could fairly be called a temptation with his gleaming eyes and teasing voice.

She sighed and had another sip of wine.

She had not called Jack to take him up on his dinner invitation, and he'd probably shrugged that one off and moved on to greener pastures. A man like Jack Millard could find plenty of other women eager to have dinner with him. Younger ones. Prettier ones. Why bother with Christina Kenley, who was past her prime and being difficult?

The next morning, with the courage of desperation, Christina called Jack's secretary and made arrangements for the dinner, which included a visit to the house to check out the kitchen and available equipment. Mrs.

Dawkins, the housekeeper, would show her around, she was told, and would also be available to help with the dinner.

On the few occasions that Christina had catered a dinner party in Philadelphia, she'd engaged the free-lance help of a couple of friends. The job finished, she'd stay the night with one or the other in town rather than driving all the way back home to the inn late at night.

The first problem with the Millard job started early on in the game. She should have guessed there would be problems. Everything concerning Jack Millard was a problem. Neither one of her friends was available to work that night. She called Dana. Dana said she'd be happy to help her out. Her roommate was having a party, but she was always giving parties and Dana didn't care about missing this one. Besides, it would still be going by the time she got back. That meant Christina couldn't ask for the use of the crummy couch in the student apartment.

At this point, Christina was ready to tear her hair out. She'd have to stay in a hotel and make it part of the expenses, but she would have to clear this with Jack first; after all, hotel accommodations were not part of a standard catering agreement. Christina called his secretary, who put her on hold for a few moments and then put her through to Jack.

"Hello, Christina," she heard him say, and her heart made a funny little leap. She had hoped to be able to avoid talking to him just because it would be easier on her nerves, which had a mind of their own. They reacted to his deep voice; it was such a sexy, seductive voice.

"Hello, Jack," she said, trying to sound businesslike. "I'm afraid we have a small problem."

"My secretary told me, yes. No problem at all." His tone was decisive. He told her it was nonsense for her to stay at a hotel. He had a perfectly good guest room with a private bathroom in his house and it had not occurred to him that she was making arrangements to stay somewhere else.

Christina's hand was clammy and she felt a moment of panic. Stay at his house? Was he crazy? Was she crazy? Was she overreacting?

She dragged in a deep breath, closing her eyes briefly. She *was* overreacting. His suggestion made perfect sense. There was nothing to do but to accept the situation as it was. It was not professional to bail out now. So she accepted his offer in as calm a manner as she could manage and politely tried to terminate the conversation. She heard the humor in his voice as he wished her a good day, and she gritted her teeth.

She could handle it. It was business after all. Just business.

Sure it was. She put the phone down with a dire sense of dread. He was reeling her in ever closer. Next week Wednesday she would be in his home, not only in the kitchen cooking dinner, but staying the night under his roof.

To her relief, he was not at home the day she came to his house to scout out the location. It was a beautiful old house with sweeping lawns dotted by large trees now losing their autumn-colored leaves. It was large and impressive and probably had some ghosts haunting its attics.

Inside, it was equally impressive, with glowing Persian rugs and an eclectic mixture of antique, contemporary and Oriental furniture. In spite of the obvious luxury of it all, the place looked inviting and comfortable, and quite lived-in. Well, she reminded herself, the man had two teenage children. No doubt quite a bit of living went on in the house.

Mrs. Dawkins, the housekeeper, was a friendly, motherly woman in her sixties, who showed her the spacious and well-equipped kitchen. Preparing a meal for twenty wouldn't be a problem. Mrs. Dawkins showed her the dining room, the china, the crystal, the silverware, saying she could take care of preparing the table if Christina would like.

They were talking about details over coffee and apple pie when Jack came into the kitchen, surprising them both. Christina felt her heart trip and stumble at the sight of him. Dressed in business suit and tie, he radiated energy and masculine confidence. She felt an instant anger at herself. She didn't want to have such a strong reaction to him, but she seemed incapable of controlling it. It was just there.

"Wasn't expecting you," Mrs. Dawkins offered.

"Wasn't expecting myself, either," Jack returned, "but a meeting was canceled and I thought perhaps it would be a good idea to drop by and see if you two can get along." He looked meaningfully at the coffee and pie, taking in the obviously friendly atmosphere prevailing in the kitchen. Then he glanced over at Christina.

"How are you?" he asked, his dark gaze locking with hers, looking into her soul, or so it seemed.

"I'm fine, thank you," she said, her voice not quite steady. Her heart was going crazy. It wasn't fair. Why was this happening to her? This wasn't what she needed.

"I've looked at the menu you sent me. It's excellent. I've signed the contract and had it sent back to you."

"Thank you."

"Would you like a cup of coffee, Mr. Millard?" Mrs. Dawkins held out the coffeepot.

"Please." He pulled out a chair and sat down, unbuttoning his suit jacket. "Did you put away the photos I left on the coffee table last night?" he asked her. "I need to take them back to the office."

She poured the coffee. "I put them on your desk. I'll get them."

Mrs. Dawkins left the kitchen and Christina looked at Jack's hand as he lifted the cup to take a drink. A strong brown hand, accentuated by the white cuffs of his shirt.

"I forgot to ask you if you meant for me to be serving the meal, as well," she said, glancing up at him.

He arched his brows. "Yes, of course, as you do at the inn. Do you mind?"

"No, that's fine. And in terms of clothes, I'll wear just what I do at the inn. Or do you prefer something a little more formal than dress pants and a blouse?"

He frowned slightly. "I was thinking you might want to wear a short skirt and a frilly little apron, you know..." Her outraged expression made him laugh out loud. "Lighten up, Christina. I'm joking."

She felt silly. "Sorry," she muttered. "My husband..." She stopped herself.

"Your husband what?"

She shrugged. "He used to tell me what to wear. He never liked the way I looked."

"Really? He must have been blind." He smiled. "I like the way you look just fine."

"Thank you." She couldn't think of anything else to say, wondering what he'd thought of the frumpy robe and slippers he'd seen her in.

"As a matter of fact," he went on casually, "I keep thinking about just how much I like the way you look."

She slanted him a withering glance, which only made him laugh again. But she was prevented from saying anything further by Mrs. Dawkins's return to the kitchen with the envelope of photographs.

Jack took the pictures out and spread them around on the table. "What do you think, Christina?" His voice was perfectly even again.

They were pictures of a magnificent old colonial country house in a springtime setting—blooming azaleas, flowering dogwoods. It was made of stone, had shuttered windows and a large veranda, but it had an undeniable aura of neglect.

"It's beautiful. Whose house is it?"

"The company bought it. It's an old country estate, about half an hour out of town. It's being restored and remodeled and we'll use it as a retreat for executives and overseas business clients, and for friends and family."

"It's magnificent."

He frowned. "It needs a lot of work, though. And the furnishing and interior decorating will be a major job."

"Yes. Should be fun to do, a big house like that."

He looked up. "Who furnished and decorated the inn?"

"Oh, my mother and I did it ourselves. We didn't have professional help." She smiled, remembering. "It was great. We went to auctions and flea markets and antique shops and just gathered and collected whatever we thought would fit. Each room was decorated individually."

"It looks very well put together," he said. "You must have very good creative instincts." He met her gaze and his mouth tilted upward at the corners. "Not that I'm surprised, having tasted your food."

She felt warm all over. Many people had complimented her, but somehow to hear Jack say those words had an impact way beyond the reasonable. She was a fool to be taken in by him so easily. "I loved doing it," she said, looking down at one of the pictures to avoid his gaze.

"You want more coffee?" Mrs. Dawkins asked.

Christina shook her head. "I've had two already, thanks. I really have to get back home." She pushed her chair away from the table and smiled at Mrs. Dawkins. "I'm glad you'll be here to help with the dinner and that you don't mind my taking over your kitchen."

Mrs. Dawkins laughed. "Heavens no. Don't worry about a thing. It'll be fun."

Jack accompanied her to the door and helped her with her coat. A grouping of large, framed black-and-white photographs decorated one of the walls of the spacious hall. Christina had noticed them as she entered the house earlier; they were hard to miss. They depicted a boy and a girl at play in various settings, displaying a variety of emotions. The photos were clearly the work of an artist.

"These are wonderful pictures," Christina said. "Are these your children when they were little?"

"Yes." He smiled. "My wife was a photographer."

She buttoned her coat as she took in that information. "She must have been very talented. They're beautiful."

"Yes. After all these years, I still enjoy looking at them." He handed her her scarf. "I appreciate your taking on the job, Christina. My guests are friends as well as clients and I'd like to reciprocate the hospitality they've offered me over the years."

"I'll do my best," she said lightly.

His mouth curved with amusement. "I know you will."

She swallowed, wondering why this man could disturb her equilibrium just by looking at her. "I'll see you next week Wednesday," she said.

"I'm looking forward to it." He did not touch her, made no move to kiss her. He simply opened the door for her. She wasn't sure if she was relieved or disappointed.

She drove back home, having the odd premonition that some secret force was taking over her life.

* * *

Anne Marie called that afternoon and Christina sagged into a chair, resigning herself to hear another wailing session about Jason the Terrible. Anne Marie was not having a good time lately.

Jason had taken her car, she said, and had been gone for three hours. He was only thirteen and was going to hell in a hand basket. He refused to do his homework, had been expelled for cursing at one of his teachers and using foul language.

"I don't know what's wrong with him! He's had therapy for months and it's doing absolutely no good! He's going nuts! He's smoking cigarettes, he trashed his room, he's broken his window and he hasn't had a shower in three days."

Christina felt numb with shock. The stressful time her sister was going through was a concern—had been a concern. It was hard to understand that her outgoing, lovable nephew was turning into a delinquent, and destroying himself along with his family.

Up to now, she had thought her sister, who was the consummate Earth Mother of four perfectly lovely children, had been exaggerating a little, had been overly concerned about what might be called the normal teenage behavior of her son. What she was describing was no longer normal.

Something was wrong.

And she couldn't think of a thing to do to help her sister.

Wednesday arrived and Christina drove to Philadelphia, picked Dana up at her apartment and together they went on to the Millard mansion.

"I told you he was filthy rich," Dana whispered as they drove up the circular drive. "Look at this house! It's awesome!" She gazed at it in wonder for a moment, then grinned at Christina. "But what's really important, of course, is that he is a good person." She said it in an exaggerated imitation of Christina's own words—words she had said many times in one context or another to teach her daughter about what really mattered about people. It wasn't their social status, their religion, their race, the work they did, but what kind of people they were: their character and values, their behavior toward others.

Christina glowered at her daughter as she parked the car. Dana gave her a wide-eyed, innocent look.

"Mr. Millard is a good person, Mom. And *very* nice."

"And you base that judgment on one conversation with him sitting under a tree?" She turned off the engine and took the key out of the ignition.

Dana tilted her chin. "I have good instincts about people." She paused. "Actually, I think I must be a little psychic. I just *know*. I *sense* it. Mr. Millard is a very good, nice person."

Christina groaned. "Oh, please, Dana."

"And I also sense that he might be interested in you," Dana intoned.

"He is interested in my food," Christina said flatly.

"And your legs. You've got great legs."

"He's never seen my legs! Will you shut up, Dana?" She climbed out of the car and slammed the door with a little more force than was necessary. Dana looked repentant, but remained obediently silent like the good daughter she was.

For the next few hours, Christina busied herself with the preparations for the meal for Jack's guests with the able help of Mrs. Dawkins and Dana. She'd seen Jack only briefly after he'd come home from work and gone into the kitchen to say hello.

They were arranging the first-course plates when a young girl entered the kitchen with a flat box containing the remains of a pizza. She had a long curtain of dark hair, big brown eyes and a mouth full of braces. Jack's daughter, Nicole, Christina thought with an odd little flip of her heart. The girl sported the teenage uniform of oversize jeans and oversize heavy shirt that kept every possible feature of her body hidden in the folds of fabric. Finding no space on the counter, she deposited the box on a chair, which did not meet with Mrs. Dawkins's approval.

"Put that thing straight in the container outside, honey," she admonished.

"There's one piece left. I'll wrap it up. Matt says he'll have it for breakfast."

Mrs. Dawkins groaned. "What is this world coming to? Pizza for breakfast."

Dana laughed and gave the girl a knowing look. "I love pizza for breakfast." She took a tray of glasses filled with ice water and went to the dining room. Nicole dutifully wrapped up the triangle of pizza and put it in the refrigerator, all the while looking at Christina with open curiosity.

"Are you the lady who sent the cops after my dad?" she asked as she picked up the empty pizza box.

Christina smiled. "Yes, I am. And you must be Nicole."

The girl nodded, her eyes bright. "It was so cool," she said, chuckling. "You really thought he was a *criminal*?"

"Nicole!" Mrs. Dawkins was not amused.

Nicole laughed. "I'm sorry, I didn't mean to be rude."

Christina couldn't help smiling. "That's all right. And my name is Christina."

"I'll have to call you Mrs. Something. My dad says I shouldn't call grown-ups by their first names. It's not appropriate." She rolled her eyes as if she thought being appropriate was the epitome of stuffiness.

"I see. Well, you can call me Mrs. Kenley." Christina wondered what Nicole would think of the appropriateness of her father's inviting Christina into the bathroom to keep him company while he sat naked in the tub eating a sandwich. It probably would not fit her image of him as a fuddy-duddy.

Dana came back into the kitchen and Christina introduced the two. "I love your hair," Nicole told Dana, whose long blond hair had been done up in a French braid. "Did you do it yourself?" Dana nodded and Nicole sighed longingly. "I keep trying it, but it won't work."

"It takes a lot of practice," Dana admitted. She glanced at Christina, a sudden spark in her bright blue eyes. "But my mom knows how to do it, and she'll be here in the morning, so if you're nice to her, I'll bet she'll do it for you before you go to school."

Nicole gave Christina a wide-eyed look. "Would you really?"

It was clear to Christina that Dana had seen an opportunity and grasped it; her suggestion was not nearly as innocent as it appeared on the surface. Having no choice but to go along, she smiled at Nicole. "Sure."

"Cool!"

Mrs. Dawkins had had enough apparently, because she took Nicole by the shoulders and propelled her in the direction of the back door. "Get rid of that box, honey, and skedaddle out of here. We've got work to do."

And so they had.

Dana helped Christina serve the food. Jack was sitting at the head of the table in an evening jacket, looking stunningly handsome and sophisticated. A woman was sitting on his left, thirtyish, with red hair and impressive cleavage. She seemed a cheery type, laughing often and paying much attention to Jack, who also laughed a lot.

Christina found it hard not to look at her. Her flaming hair, her bubbly laughter and her heaving bosom all screamed for attention.

Back in the kitchen after serving another course, Dana grinned at Christina and leaned close. "Silicone, I'll bet," she said under her breath.

Christina made a noncommittal noise. The woman annoyed her with her flamboyance. Jack annoyed her by apparently enjoying her flamboyance. Although, whenever she entered the room, his gaze moved to her, acknowledging her presence, a smile in his eyes.

Everything went smoothly, everything was delicious and the guests complimented her profusely. She had, in fact, outdone herself. She was also exhausted.

Her duties finished, she retreated to the room Mrs. Dawkins had shown her on her arrival that afternoon and took a long, relaxing bath in the well-appointed bathroom, pouring a liberal amount of fragrant bath oil into the water.

She'd dried off, put on a nightgown and was brushing her hair when Dana came in to say good-night.

"It went great, Mom!" she said, almost jubilant. "I think everybody was really, really impressed."

"I'm glad. Thanks for helping out."

"Oh, it was fun. I liked it." Dana hugged her. "I'm leaving now. Mr. Millard got me a taxi. Oh, Mrs. Dawkins is bringing you up a cup of hot chocolate. I told her you'd like that."

"Thanks. I'd love one." She kissed Dana's warm cheek.

Only moments after Dana had left, there was another knock on the door.

"Come in," she called, putting down her hairbrush and standing.

It wasn't Mrs. Dawkins who came in, but Jack, a cup of cocoa in his hand. Her heart lurched, and she quickly reached for her robe. Not that she was exposed in any way; her white cotton nightgown, though feminine and pretty, was quite unrevealing.

"I intercepted this from Mrs. Dawkins," he said. "As long as you're still up, I thought I'd let you know you were wonderful this evening and the food was magnificent. You are a very talented person."

"Thank you." She pulled her robe on and knotted the belt. She found the smile in his eyes unnerving. He handed her the cup and she took it from him, saying thank you again, feeling unaccountably nervous. He was so tall and broad and overpowering in his evening clothes and she felt like a vulnerable little girl in her night things. She wished she had on a sexy evening gown and very high heels and diamonds in her ears. And a modest amount of cleavage. Her hands shook and she put the cup on the dresser.

He made no move to go. He searched her face. "Relax," he said quietly. He moved a step closer, reached out with one hand and stroked her hair in a brief, fleeting caress.

"Don't," she said tightly and took a step away from him. "You shouldn't be here, in this room."

His mouth quirked. "You're fully covered from head to toe. You're perfectly decent." He paused. "Also very kissable."

She moved back another step. "Is that why you gave me this job? So you could lure me into your house and seduce me?"

His eyes widened a fraction and then he laughed—a warm, humorous laugh that mortified and enraged her at the same time.

She couldn't believe it. He was laughing!

And then he pulled her into his arms and hugged her close. "Christina, relax! My daughter's room is right next door. My son's across the hall. There are twenty-some people downstairs. One good scream and they'll all be right here in this room." He moved a little closer, eyes intent on her face. "Do you really think I came here to *seduce* you?"

She felt like a complete idiot. "You make me nervous!" she said fiercely. "You've been looking at me all night. How do I know what you want?"

"I like looking at you," he said softly. He reached out and took her face in his hands. "And what I want is to kiss you." And he did. Thoroughly.

She tried to fight it, of course, but what defenses did she have—she whose newly discovered sexual appetite had lain dormant for so long and now demanded to be satisfied?

Rational thought and good intentions evaporated in the heat of his kiss. Her body molded itself against his as if it belonged there, flooding with warmth and need. His mouth made magic with hers.

She liked it. It was wonderful. It was awful. He was such a wonderful kisser, it scared her to death. Sanity returned and she was appalled at her own momentary abandon. She strained against his hold.

"Let me go, Jack." Her voice was oddly husky. He did as she asked and she took a trembling step away from him. "I'm not sleeping with you," she said breathlessly, just in case her unfortunate eagerness might have given him hope.

"I wasn't counting on it," he said dryly.

"Good. You'd be disappointed anyway."

"Really? And why is that?"

"You wouldn't enjoy it."

His left brow quirked up. "I wouldn't?"

"I haven't made love in years. I'm sure I've forgotten how to do it. Besides, I was never any good at it."

"And who said that?"

"My husband said that. And he should know. He had plenty of experience making love to a lot of women," she said lightly. Too lightly. She heard the artifice of it in her own tone.

He said nothing for a moment, and she moved farther away from him, feeling awkward and embarrassed by her confessions. Good Lord, why was she saying these things?

He followed her, and she felt him behind her. He put his hands on her shoulders and turned her around gently. "I'm sorry," he said softly. "I didn't mean to make you feel uncomfortable."

"I'm fine," she muttered.

"I know I'm pushing it. I know I'm probably doing this all wrong. It's just that I can't help myself."

"You can't help what?"

"The way I feel about you. You've gotten under my skin. I keep thinking about you."

And she kept thinking about him, but she wasn't going to admit it for a million dollars. She didn't really even want to admit it to herself. She fought for composure.

"Well, maybe you should get busy with other things, and it will pass," she said briefly.

"What sort of things?"

She shrugged. "Work. Junk. Other women."

"Other women?"

"Yeah. Maybe someone young and frivolous, who has lots of time on her hands." And red hair and voluminous breasts.

"I don't want somebody young and frivolous with lots of time on her hands. I want you."

Her heart turned over at his words and she regained her composure with difficulty. "You can't have me. Nobody can *have* me. I am not a possession."

His eyes narrowed slightly. "I didn't say you were, Christina," he said quietly.

"Good. And now, I think you should go downstairs and take care of your guests." She paused meaningfully. "Or I'll scream."

He gave a crooked grin. "I'm out of here. Good night, Christina, and thank you."

The next ten days were busy ones, for which Christina was grateful. Her mind was in turmoil over her feelings for Jack and the more she had to do, the better. She didn't want to fall in love. She didn't want an affair. The situation was all too complicated and rife with problems. Jack was not the right man for her.

He sent her more flowers. He called her on the phone. He wanted to see her, he said. She said she was busy. She avoided answering the phone and did not return Jack's calls. Yet at night she kept seeing the smile in his eyes, kept feeling his kiss, kept hearing his words echoing in her mind: *I want you. I want you. I want you.*

Saturday, she had a full house, and after she had cooked and served dinner, Christina helped with the cleanup because one of the kitchen helpers was home in bed with the flu. Afterward, she walked back to her cabin, exhausted. The grounds were strewn with fallen leaves and she rustled them with her feet as she walked. The November air was cold and crisp and full of the pungent scents of autumn. Taking in a deep breath, she savored the coolness, the fragrance. The sky was clear, no sign yet of the storm front that was heading their way, according to the weather forecast.

Her eyes caught a flicker of light in the distant darkness and instinctively she turned and looked again. Light where none should be, at the edge of the woods near the pond. Flickering light, as from a fire, a campfire.

She frowned. Had one of the guests built a fire without permission? Just like that? Granted, it would be romantic to sit by a fire under the stars, but the autumn chill was quite severe by November.

Pulling her jacket closer around her, she started down the path toward the fire, wondering halfway if perhaps this was not such a bright idea. It might not be guests sitting out there by the fire, but someone roaming the countryside, perhaps a hunter or someone on the loose with a gun. After all, the perimeter of her property was clearly marked. So no law-abiding, upstanding citizen would likely be trespassing.

She kept on going, finding to her surprise the faint outlines of a medium-size tent near the pond. She stopped for a moment. A tent!

She walked on, hearing music. Not rock or country or heavy metal.

Vivaldi. Vivaldi!

A man came out of the tent and she stopped, her heart in her throat. He stood silhouetted against the light of the fire and she knew who it was.

Jack.

Jack, camping out in a tent on her property. Oh, God. She wasn't sure what she was feeling—anger, relief, excitement, or a mixture of all three.

CHAPTER FIVE

SHE moved quickly now, fueled by anger. He turned around, apparently hearing her footsteps, and stood quietly waiting for her to come closer.

"I thought you'd never get here," he said calmly when she reached him.

"What do you think you're doing?" she demanded. She could not believe it was him. One moment he was the sophisticated, worldly businessman in a suit; the next he was sitting by a campfire wearing jeans.

"I think I'm camping out," he said, "in the great outdoors under a cool autumn sky."

It wasn't cool—it was cold—but she refrained from pointing that out. She clenched her hands by her side, frustrated with helpless anger. "You're on private property! You're trespassing!"

He pushed his hands into his pockets. "Really?"

"Yes, really! If you don't leave, I'll call the police!"

He gave a long-suffering sigh. "Again."

"This is not funny!" She took a deep breath and tried to calm herself. She was overreacting, she knew. "You can't camp out here. This is not a campground."

He nodded amiably. "I'm well aware of that. But there was no room at the inn, I was told. And I so wanted to see you."

"I'm flattered," she said coolly. "However, I do not want to see you."

Her words hung in the air as he gave her a long, assessing look. "This place is the perfect hideaway for you, isn't it?" he said then.

His question took her by surprise and she stared at him. "For me?" The inn was a romantic hideaway for her guests. For her it was a business. "I don't know what you mean."

"Only couples stay here. So you're safe from men, from their attentions, their advances."

She was too stunned to say a word. She'd never consciously thought of it that way. Was that what she had been doing—hiding from men?

His eyes were dark and intense. "What did that husband of yours do to you?" he asked softly.

She froze.

"Did he abuse you?"

She gave a brittle little laugh. "You mean, did he ever take a baseball bat to me? Good heavens, no. He never laid a hand on me. What makes you think that?"

His face was unreadable, and he shrugged lightly. "I was just wondering, that's all."

She took in an unsteady breath. "My marriage is none of your business," she said tightly, feeling an odd fear, wanting to put an end to this conversation, wanting him to get out of her sight.

He nodded. "Correct."

"Also, you have no business camping out on my property."

He sighed in mock despair. "But I like seeing you, being with you. You won't talk to me on the phone. You don't return my calls. What is a man to do?"

"Get over it." She planted her hands on her hips. "I want you gone. I want you to pack up your gear and leave. Now. Or I'll call the police. Do you understand?"

He nodded gravely. "I do. I'm just wondering why you are so terrified of me."

"I'm not terrified!" she snapped. "I'm just not interested!" *Liar*! said a small, secret voice inside her. She swung around and stalked back to her cabin, her heart racing, her mind in turmoil. "I mean it," she muttered under her breath. "I'll call the police."

But she knew that the police could not help her with the real problem, which was not Jack's trespassing on her property. It was his trespassing on her heart.

Jack stared up at the perfectly clear sky, admiring the beauty of the stars and the silvery moon, and thought about Christina. He'd thought about Christina a lot lately.

She was successful, smart, creative, yet there was something in her eyes that haunted him, a fearful vulnerability that seemed at odds with her confident, competent manner. There was something very soft and sweet about her, something that made him want to put his arms around her and protect her.

Protect her. He grinned at himself. Against what? She didn't seem in need of any kind of protection. She was doing just fine running her classy inn. She didn't need him or his attentions. Didn't *want* his attentions.

Something twisted in his gut. He didn't like that feeling. Was it just wounded male pride, or something else? Was it the need to... to what? To hold a woman? No, not just to hold a woman. To hold a woman who wanted him and loved him. There was a world of difference there, and he knew it.

That hollow ache in his chest again. He had not allowed himself to feel it often, because with it always came the painful longing for Sara, who'd once owned his soul. But she had died a long time ago, and he had moved on—had had to move on. He had worked hard, tried to raise his children with love and plenty of attention and to push his own needs to the background.

There hadn't been any lack of female attention in his life, and a couple of times over the years he had tried to build a relationship with a woman, but he had never succeeded in making it meaningful. There were reasons for that, he assumed, possibly within himself, but he had not wanted to analyze them at the time, and in the past couple of years he had given up hope for permanency. He was a lucky man to have had the love of a wonderful woman once. Could he possibly be so greedy as to expect to have it again?

Now he was in love and acting like a total idiot, camping out in a tent on Christina's property. It would serve him right if she sent the police after him again. And this time they'd have every right to arrest him for trespassing or stalking or whatever. He was forty-five years old and he was behaving like a besotted teenager with out-of-control hormones.

A gust of cold, damp wind chilled him. He turned back into the tent and crawled into his sleeping bag.

Christina awoke to the sound of wind and rain assaulting the trees, pounding on the roof of the cabin. Almost three, the clock said. She tossed and turned, exasperated. She needed her sleep, but the howling wind kept her awake, as did her thoughts of Jack, who surely must have packed up and left.

Then again, maybe he had not. She'd gone to bed as soon as she had delivered her tirade and had not seen him leave.

A resounding crash jerked her straight up in bed, her heart pounding wildly. A tree, that's what it was. The storm must have uprooted a tree somewhere.

She lay back down and let out a trembling sigh.

What if Jack was still out there in his tent? It was dangerous in this weather. His tent could blow over.

"Would serve him right," she muttered into the darkness. He should never have come in the first place. Anyway, he had probably left.

What if he hadn't?

She groaned, disgusted with herself. He was a big boy. He could take care of himself. It was his own fault if his tent blew over. He'd have brought his misfortunes upon himself. She was not responsible for him.

Clambering out of bed, she put on her robe and went into the kitchen. Peering out of the window proved to be useless. There was nothing but stormy, impenetrable darkness outside. If Jack was still out there in his tent, she'd never see him from the cabin.

After a few minutes of struggling fruitlessly with herself, she put on a sweat suit, rubber boots and a raincoat and went outside, carrying a big flashlight, berating herself. She was a hopeless idiot. She should have her head examined.

Leaning into the wind, she fought to keep her balance. Icy rain stung her face. Clenching her teeth, her body tense, she inched forward in the direction of the pond, peering into the darkness, praying Jack was safe and somewhere under a sturdy roof.

He wasn't. The beam from her flashlight caught the tent as it flapped and strained against the onslaught of the wind. Inside, she presumed, was Jack.

She muttered a curse under her breath. The man was an irresponsible maniac, making her venture out in this weather. She could fall and break a leg and die of exposure before anyone would find her tomorrow morning.

"Jack!" she yelled against the wind, shining her flashlight over the front of the tent. "Jack! Are you in there?"

The tent zipped open. "Are you crazy, woman?" Jack's hand shot out and he pulled her bodily into the tent. She sagged against him on top of his sleeping bag, dripping water everywhere. "Good God, Christina, what possessed you?" he ground out. "It's three in the morning!"

"I told you to leave!"

"Yes, I remember that."

He was insufferable. She didn't know how to defend herself against him. "So why didn't you?"

"Because I didn't want to."

For him it was all so simple. Water was dripping down her face. She wiped at it impatiently. She didn't know what to do with this man, how to act, what to say. He was driving her nuts.

"You can't stay outside in this weather," she said.

"I'm not outside. I'm in a tent."

She gritted her teeth. "It's storming!"

"I noticed, yes, but I'm perfectly warm and perfectly dry," he said. "I'm a very competent camper."

"Your tent might get blown away!"

"It never has before. This is a very good tent."

"A tree fell! Didn't you hear it?"

He nodded. "The ground rather thundered, didn't it?"

"Yes. What if one falls on your tent?"

He frowned. "It would be messy."

"You'd be dead!"

He nodded. "Possibly. And you wouldn't want that?"

"I don't need any dead bodies on my property!" she snapped.

He laughed. "Not good for business."

"Right."

He sighed. "For a moment, I thought you might just be concerned for me as a person, a fellow human being."

She glared at him. "Are you coming inside with me or not?"

"Your most gracious invitation is hard to turn down. Besides, I have two kids who still need me, so I suppose I'd better go to the inn."

"We're full."

He frowned again. "Really?"

"Yes!" It was even the truth.

"So where will I go?"

"You'll have to stay at my cabin."

"Ah," he said meaningfully. "Why didn't you say so in the first place?"

She glowered at him. "Don't get any ideas."

He gave a devilish grin. "I can't help it. They come on their own accord, those ideas of mine."

He was infuriating. She wiped a strand of wet hair out of her face and fixed him with a cold stare. He sighed and glanced at his sleeping bag, which now was thoroughly soaked.

"You've made a mess of everything in here, so I really have no choice but to go back with you."

"So now it's all my fault?"

"You did soak my sleeping bag," he pointed out truthfully. "So you really do owe me a dry place to sleep, I would say."

"*Owe* you?" She caught the smirk on his face. "Oh, shut up," she muttered.

He laughed and then his warm mouth brushed across her cold lips. "Relax, Christina," he whispered. "I was trying to rile you."

And he had succeeded nicely. Stupid her. He'd quickly discovered how to push her buttons, and she was allowing him to. She drew away from him, which wasn't easy as there wasn't much room to maneuver in. She watched in silence as he pulled a rain poncho over his head, put on old sneakers and grabbed his duffel bag.

"All right, let's go."

He put one arm firmly around her as they negotiated the way back to her cabin with the wind in their backs and the rain pouring over them in a torrent.

Once inside the cabin, he told her she should get into some warm and dry clothes while he would stir up the fire in the wood stove.

"My plans exactly," she said, not liking the idea he was telling her what to do. "Only don't bother with the fire. I'm going to sleep."

His brows arched. "Really?" A blinding flash of lightning, followed by a horrendous crack of thunder, seemed to accentuate his remark.

Saying nothing, she turned her back on him and went into her bedroom and stripped off her sodden clothes. She'd have liked to take a hot shower, but with the lightning outside it seemed not a good idea. Instead of her nightclothes, she pulled on a blue sweat suit and thick socks. Returning to the living room, she found the fire blazing.

"You'd better get into some dry clothes yourself," she suggested, knowing he was as wet and muddy as she had been.

She gave him a towel, and while he was in the bathroom, she found a pillow and a comforter and put them on the sofa. By the time he emerged from the bathroom wearing a clean sweat suit, she had two mugs of hot chocolate ready, liberally laced with rum. It would only be childish to go to bed now and pretend she could sleep.

He reached for her hand and gently drew her down on the sofa next to him. "Now, are you warm?" he asked.

"I'm fine," she said, slipping her hand out of his.

"It's very nice and cozy in here," he commented, glancing around with obvious contentment. "Thank you for coming to rescue me from the elements. It's more than I deserved."

"I should have let you perish."

"Right. But I'm so glad you didn't. You are a good woman."

"Oh, be quiet," she muttered, and sipped her hot cocoa.

He laughed softly. "I like you, Christina. Why does that frighten you?"

"I'm not afraid. I'm just . . . suspicious."

His brows arched in surprise. "Suspicious? About what?"

"About why you are in such hot pursuit of me," she said bravely. So there, she'd said it. It was the truth after all.

"Is that so strange?" he asked.

She shrugged. "You're rich, successful, handsome and available. You could have a twenty-five-year-old with perky breasts."

He rolled his eyes. "I'm not in love with a twenty-five-year-old with perky breasts. I'm not *interested* in a twenty-five-year-old with perky breasts. I'm interested in you."

It sounded good. It sounded flattering. It frightened her. "I can't imagine why."

"Why *not*?"

"I'm old, I'm ordinary, I'm not gorgeous, I have no money."

"I'm older than you, you're not ordinary, I don't care about gorgeous and I'm not interested in your money or lack thereof. How's that?"

She sighed. "What do you want with me?"

His gaze didn't leave her face. "I want to get to know you better. I want to spend time with you, talk to you, make you laugh." He paused. "And to be honest, when the time is right, I want to make love to you."

She stiffened. "No, you don't."

"Oh, yes, I do."

"You don't know what lurks under these clothes," she muttered darkly.

He laughed. "I'd like to find out."

"No, you don't."

He quirked a brow. "What's wrong? You look pretty good to me."

"That's what you think."

"So what's wrong?"

"I'm forty-two years old. I have stretch marks. My breasts droop. I'm on the brink of menopause."

"No kidding," he said deadpan. "Who'd have guessed?"

"It's not funny."

He looked solemn. "It's a nightmare."

"Exactly."

"You're trying to scare me off?"

"Yes," she said.

He gave her a quizzical look. "What did you think I expected? The body of a twenty-year-old? Perky breasts, flat stomach, no cellulite?"

"I do *not* have cellulite!"

He grinned. "See, it's not so bad after all."

"You're making fun of me."

"Yes. Do you think in the heat of passion I'm going to see your stretch marks?"

"Yes," she said promptly.

He laughed. "You obviously have no idea what happens when I'm in the throes of passion. I think perhaps you should try it out. It might be a very enlightening experience."

"You're making fun of me," she muttered for the second time.

"You make it such a satisfactory endeavor," he murmured. "What are you afraid of, Christina?"

"Of ending up on the Oprah show."

"What?"

She sighed. "You know, silly older women besotted with handsome rich men who use them for their own evil purposes."

"Like what?"

She shrugged. "Who knows? Drug smuggling or some other immoral or illegal activities. And the poor besotted fools of women are so hypnotized by money and sex, they do anything the men want them to do."

"You really know how to stroke a man's ego," he said dryly. "I thought I had convinced you of my upstanding moral character by now."

"I'm never going to stroke a man's ego again in my entire life, or any lives coming after this one," she stated flatly.

"Ah!" he said meaningfully.

"What do you mean, ah?" she asked.

"I take it your husband's ego needed a lot of stroking?"

"Yes."

"And you, the dutiful wife, stroked yourself silly."

She glared at him. "I *know* I was stupid. You don't have to point it out to me."

He nodded. "Sorry. And now, I understand, you are no longer stupid. No more men, no more ego stroking, no more love, no more sex. What a wonderful life!"

"Right. It's calm and peaceful and very relaxing."

"So is sitting in a rocking chair on the porch."

She wanted to throw her cocoa at him, but it was finished. She wanted to yell at him, but it was so undignified. Instead, she walked out of the room and into the kitchen.

He followed her.

"I'm sorry," he said. "I didn't mean to make you angry."

"Yes, you did," she said through clenched teeth. "I know what you want. You want some torrid affair with me and your tender male ego can't stand it that I'm not interested. But let me assure you that it's just as well. I'm not one of those sexy, passionate women who can drive a man crazy with lust, so why not save yourself the effort?'' He laughed, an honest rumble of a laugh, and she glared at him, outraged. ''I'm trying to be honest,'' she said. ''Don't laugh at me!''

''I'm not laughing *at* you. I don't think that you yourself are the best judge of whether or not you're sexy and can drive a man crazy with desire.''

She said nothing. She felt hopeless, trapped against the counter with him towering in front of her.

''You don't scare me off, you know,'' he said softly. ''Are you really worried about making love?''

It was so crazy. Here she was, a mature woman in her forties, afraid of sex as if she were a timid virgin. It was really pathetic. And here was this sexy man interested in her, trying to rescue her from sexual stagnation. She should be grateful, really. She gave a long sigh. There was no fooling him and she shouldn't even try.

''I'm terrified. Especially because I think you're probably very, very good.''

He laughed softly. ''I'll teach you. Step by step, stroke by stroke, kiss by kiss.''

''No,'' she said.

He sighed. ''Okay.''

She met his eyes in surprise. ''Just like that?''

The corners of his mouth quirked. ''What else?''

She bit her lip and shrugged. ''Nothing.'' There was something very special about Jack Millard, and it was harder and harder to ignore. It was harder and harder not to fall for his charm and just let him sweep her off her feet.

Was she crazy? Was she naive? Why would a man like Jack be interested in her? She heard the howling of the wind outside and shivered.

He put his arms around her. ''Let me just hold you,'' he said. ''No hanky-panky, I promise.''

Against her better judgment, she allowed him to simply hold her. It was a wonderful feeling. It was a terrifying feeling. Her head was on his shoulder, her cheek against the warm hollow of his neck. She smelled the faint, manly scent of him, felt an odd, light feeling in her head.

For a short while, they just stood there. Then he guided her back to the warmth of the fire, pulling her down next to him on the sofa.

"Tell me about your husband," he said quietly. "You said he did not physically abuse you, but there are other forms of abuse. What did he do to you?"

She sighed, fighting for a moment the urge to say she didn't want to talk about Peter. It ruined her sense of comfort, but it was probably just as well. She shrugged lightly.

"Nothing terribly dramatic. He always criticized me, always put me down. I could never do anything right. He didn't respect me. He didn't...*value* me."

She didn't like the way she answered the question. It sounded as if she considered herself to be a helpless, victimized female. She was quite aware of the truth about being a doormat: People can't step on you if you don't lie down. She swallowed.

"The worst of it," she went on, "was that I *allowed* him to treat me this way. I didn't stand up to him."

"Why not?"

"It was so...subtle at first, you know. It didn't seem a big deal. And in the beginning, I thought that maybe he was right about some things—my hair, my clothes. He was a few years older and more sophisticated than I was. He never yelled or hurt me physically. It was very insidious. It got worse, of course, this slowly chipping away at my self-esteem, and I kept on not doing anything about it."

When she'd become pregnant with Dana, their life together had deteriorated even more quickly. She had been sick most of the nine months, getting into an intimate relationship with the toilet bowl. Utterly miserable, she had dragged herself through the days, not caring what she looked like, her hair lifeless and hanging limply around her face. She couldn't be bothered putting any makeup on—the toilet bowl didn't care.

Peter had not been sympathetic. He hadn't married her, he said, so she could become a slob. He had no sympathy for her constant nausea. After all, didn't most women have to go through that? It was part of the deal and she should grow up and live with it.

However, Peter certainly wasn't going to grow up and live with it—that much became all too obvious. He stayed away night after night and when he was home he took to sleeping in the guest room so she wouldn't wake him up. She slept restlessly, woke up early, feeling sick.

After the baby was born, the situation between them did not improve, although he seemed to be interested in the baby for a while, being delighted to show her off to his friends. Dana was a beautiful baby, and he bragged about how she looked like him as if he were the only one responsible for her creation.

"Peter was always worried about what people would think about him and about me, about his image," she told Jack, sparing him the more miserable details.

Jack studied her face. "How did he criticize you? About what?"

"About everything. My clothes, my hair, my housekeeping, my conversation." She laughed softly. "My cooking."

"Your *cooking*?"

She sighed melodramatically. "I was a failure all the way around. You have no idea how inadequate I was. I didn't even brush my teeth right, he said."

Jack didn't laugh.

She smiled at him. "Lighten up, Jack. It was a long time ago. I've since learned I'm quite adequate, not to say brilliant, in various parts of my life."

His mouth quirked. "Good. I like brilliant women."

"Mmm."

"Let's play a game," he said, changing the subject so abruptly she almost laughed.

"A game?"

"A mind game." The laughter was back in his eyes.

"A mind game. I'm playing no mind games with you."

He sighed. "You're no fun, you know. You won't let me play with your body, and you won't let me play with your mind."

"You're nuts," she said coolly.

He nodded in agreement. "But quite harmless."

She saw the amused slant of his mouth, the dark glint in his eyes, and knew he was not harmless at all. He was irresistible, winning her over with his charm.

"What kind of mind game?" she finally asked, curious.

"Mind travel. A game of fantasy and pretense."

She looked at him suspiciously. "You're kidding me."

"Nope. You'll like it. It's fun."

"What do we do?"

"You'll see. Now, just relax and close your eyes."

Relax? She wasn't sure if she was capable of relaxing with him sitting next to her. And with her eyes closed, too.

"Do I have to close my eyes?"

"Yes."

"Is this some sort of kinky seduction routine?"

He laughed. "You are suspicious, aren't you?" He lifted his hands in the air. "Nothing kinky, hands off, promise."

"And what will you do while I sit here all relaxed with my eyes closed?"

"I'll talk to you and ask you questions, that's all. I won't move even an inch and I won't touch you."

"How do I know you're telling the truth?"

"You don't know. You'll have to trust me. But either we're going to play the game, or I'm going to kiss you silly and make passionate love to you right here in front of the fire. Take your pick."

"I'll play the game," she said promptly and he sighed.

"If that's the best you can do, let's do it. Make yourself comfortable and close your eyes."

She made herself comfortable and closed her eyes.

"Breathe quietly and relax."

She did as he told her, and it wasn't hard to relax.

"Take a deep breath and blow it out slowly."

She took a deep breath and blew it out slowly. He had a wonderful voice, very comforting. He told her to take deep breaths a couple more times. Very relaxing indeed.

"Now, in your mind, look up and see a summer sky. Describe it to me."

She told him it was very, very blue, with wonderful white clouds floating gently in a breeze.

"Feel yourself fly," he suggested, and she did, allowing herself to be guided by his voice.

She floated high in the sky, and it really was quite amazing how relaxing it felt. On and on, flying, floating, seeing the world below on a May morning. She told him what she saw, playing the game, almost believing it, feeling wonderfully free.

From afar she heard his voice. "Slowly now, float back to earth."

"I don't want to," she murmured. "It's so nice up here."

He laughed softly. "It will be nice on earth. You'll find a magic spot. Feel yourself gently float down, feet first, gently, gently." He guided her down slowly. "Feel your feet touch the ground. Look around and see where you have landed. Tell me what you see in your magic spot."

"I'm on a beach," she said, "and there are palm trees and the sea is very blue. There's a house nearby, on the beach. It's white with a big veranda and behind it there are hills and forests. A rain forest, I think." She heard birds, heard the rushing of the waves. "It's very peaceful, very beautiful."

"Are you alone?" he asked.

"Yes. No. There is someone else but I can't see him. He's at the edge of the woods, between the trees, but I can't make him out. I'm trying."

"Do you know him?"

"I'm not sure. I think I do, but...I don't know."

"All right. You're going to take a walk along the beach. Look up at the sky. What do you see?"

She told him what she saw, and he told her to float back up into the air, and she said she didn't want to leave, but he gently made the suggestion again and she did. After which he guided her back to Pennsylvania, to her cabin. And she opened her eyes and found herself sitting on her own sofa with Jack studying her, and for a moment she felt vaguely disoriented.

She let out a deep sigh. "Good grief, that almost felt real."

He laughed. "Ah, the power of the imagination."

"It's probably all those travel magazines I read and my great wish to laze in the sun on a beach and spend the day reading and swimming and basically doing absolutely nothing at all."

He smiled. "How do you feel?"

"Quite relaxed, actually. You must have done this before."

"Lots of times, in all kinds of variations. Sara and I often did it with the children. They loved it."

"Sara...your wife?"

"Yes." A slight pause. "She was in a serious car accident when she was a teenager and was in a lot of pain for a long time. She had a nurse who worked with her, using this guided imagery, and it helped with the pain. It's a useful technique, but it can also just be fun. You should have heard some of the stuff my kids came up with." He rose to his feet and put another log on the fire. "You look very sleepy."

"I am." It was suddenly hard to keep her eyes open. "I'm going to bed."

"I think the storm is easing."

She listened. It was still raining, but the rumbling of thunder had faded into the distance. "Yes, good." She struggled to her feet. "I hope you'll be all right on the sofa. It doesn't pull out into a bed, I'm afraid."

"I'll be fine."

She wished him good-night and went into her own room and, miraculously, fell instantly asleep. She dreamed of lying on a tropical beach without any clothes on, of Jack stroking her body, saying she was beautiful, saying she was making him crazy with desire. Saying he wanted to make love to her.

That scared her so much, she woke up. Her heart was beating fast, and for a moment she lay still, remembering the dream.

Something was seriously wrong with her if even in her dreams she was scared of making love. Millions of women with stretch marks made love all over the world. Millions of women with droopy breasts made love all over the world. What was the matter with her? Was she nothing more than a body?

She groaned. She was neurotic. She was a nut case.

The smell of coffee distracted her from her self-flagellation. Coffee. Jack. He was here, in her house. There was a man in her house making coffee. What a luxury! If he made breakfast, too, she'd be in seventh heaven.

She scrambled out of bed and stumbled into the bathroom, feeling dangerously groggy after only a few hours of sleep.

After a quick shower, she felt marginally revived, but still in serious need of caffeine. She found Jack in the living room, reading the morning paper in front of the wood stove. Wearing jeans and a sweater, his feet up on a stool, a cup of coffee by his side, he looked comfortable and relaxed, as if he spent his mornings here every day...as if he belonged.

She felt an odd little ache in her chest. He looked so good sitting there. Wouldn't it be nice to wake up in the morning, finding a man in your house and the coffee made?

Fantasies were for dreamers. She'd lived with a man once, and it was enough for a lifetime.

Jack smiled up at her. "Good morning, Christina. Did you manage to get some sleep?"

"I did, yes. Thank you."

He came to his feet. "I'll pour you some coffee and make us some breakfast—if you'll allow me. How about an omelet?"

How could she possibly resist this man? He didn't even expect her to wait on him hand and foot.

So he made them breakfast and it was quite amazingly pleasant to sit there with him in her small kitchen, eating and talking, and she knew she was lost.

She was lost when an hour later he kissed her goodbye. He was a wonderful kisser and she felt totally transported. Her body felt wonderful—alive and joyous with her blood singing and her heart dancing and her feet floating. Then he stopped kissing her and held her close for just a few moments before drawing back a little and looking into her eyes.

"Christina?"

"Yes?" She saw no laughter in his eyes now, only a dark intensity that made her heart skip a beat.

"You know there is something special between us," he said softly. "Shall we give it a chance?"

CHAPTER SIX

HER heart was pounding frantically and it was hard to breathe. There was something special between them—between him, the rich, handsome man, so charming and sexy; and her, the middle-aged divorcée so scared to death of losing her sanity, of ending up on *Oprah*.

"Shall we give it a chance?" he repeated.

She gave a desperate little moan. "Why do you have to be so rich?" she wailed. "Why do you have to be so nice and good-looking?" And so damned sexy, she added silently.

"It's a burden I have to live with," he said deadpan, "but you're the first one to complain about it. Would you rather have me be poor and fat and ugly? I could try to work on that, if it would help."

She sighed. "Would you do that for me?"

He nodded. "I'll give all my money away. I'll eat greasy food every day and gain a hundred pounds. I'll have plastic surgery to give me a weak chin and a crooked nose. You can give me a job as a dishwasher. Would you consider getting to know me then?"

She groaned, and then she was laughing. And he was laughing.

"I'll make you a deal," he said.

She frowned suspiciously. "What deal?"

"You don't have to change for me. Not a single hair, if I don't have to change for you. Fair?"

She felt a little ashamed. Here was this perfectly charming, handsome man who had money to boot, a man women would kill for, and she was complaining.

"I'm sorry," she offered, her doubts, however, still there. Getting to know Jack was a risk—a situation full of danger and excitement and it filled her with fear as well as a secret longing.

If you never take a risk, you'll lead a stagnant life. She'd read that somewhere. Stagnant. It made her think of putrid ponds.

Her life was not exactly a putrid pond, but she certainly could use a little excitement. She *deserved* a little excitement. And Monday-night bingo in a Florida retirement community wasn't what she had in mind.

He kissed her. "I want to spend time with you, talk with you, laugh with you," he whispered in her ear. "I want to know what you think and what you feel and I want to make wonderful, passionate love with you."

Her heart made a crazy leap at the thought of making wonderful, passionate love with Jack. She thought of what it would be like to have a man in her life again, someone in her bed, someone who'd be there every day, and she felt panic rise like a hot water geyser. She couldn't help it. It simply overwhelmed her. She'd once had a man in her life and it had been a nightmare. The dark shadows of that experience still lurked in hidden corners of her consciousness.

She needed her space, her freedom.

She needed air to breathe. She sucked in a deep gulp.

She didn't want anybody too close. She drew out of his embrace.

"What's wrong?" he asked.

"I'm not good at relationships," she said shakily. "I...I need my..."

"Independence?"

She nodded, relieved he understood. "Yes."

"We can have a relationship without your losing your independence. Your independence is something I like about you."

She smiled at that, wondering if he might just be a perfect man. "Good, because I worked hard for it and I'm never giving it up."

His mouth curved in a half smile. "Consider me duly warned. Now, anything else you're worried about?"

She closed her eyes and sighed. "I feel like I'm jumping off a cliff," she muttered.

"I'll hold your hand and we'll jump together," he offered, "and then we'll spread our wings and fly away into bliss."

She opened her eyes and looked at him. "You're crazy."

"About you." His eyes gleamed darkly. "And now there's something else we need to discuss."

"What?"

"Making love."

She said nothing.

"One day or night," he went on, his voice carrying a note of drama, "we're going to find ourselves overcome with passion, wanting to make unbridled love."

She swallowed hard. "Possibly," she corrected. "I'm not making any promises." Who was she fooling?

His mouth twitched. "Trust me, we'll get there."

"You are so sure of yourself."

"And of you." No smugness in his voice, just a calm reassurance. She liked it.

He lowered his face a little and kissed her, a fleeting, sensuous brushing of his lips over hers.

"There's something I want you to know," he said, no teasing in his voice. "Making love is a risky business these days, but I don't want you to worry about making love with me, not on any account." His eyes were steady, his face serious. "I'm a responsible person, Christina. You're quite safe with me."

She nodded, feeling a wave of gratitude and of something else—a warm, wonderful feeling ... of being cared for, of mattering.

"Thank you." And then she told him he didn't have to worry about her, either, because she had made sure. Peter's infidelities had hurt her, but they'd frightened her even more.

Jack smiled into her eyes, humor back in his face. "And having dealt with that, I am going to go to my office and try not to think about you, which is going to be extremely difficult." His mouth trailed kisses across her cheek to her ear. "Just for the record," he whispered, "just so you're very clear about this—you are driving me quite crazy with passion." He kissed her with a fierceness that left nothing to the imagination, then released her abruptly and stalked away.

Christina let out a long sigh. She was driving him crazy with passion. Oh boy, she, a woman past forty! A woman with crow's-feet!

It was time for a serious talk with herself. Christina looked at herself in the mirror and tried not to see the fine lines around her mouth and eyes. It wasn't that hard, really. After all, they weren't the Grand Canyon and she wasn't eighty ... yet.

Neither was she an ugly witch. Actually, she looked good. Her eyes were shiny, her cheeks a bit flushed, her hair sexily tousled. She was slim and healthy and what was the matter with her anyway, to worry about such superficial things? Wasn't she mature enough to know better? She should be ashamed of herself.

There was something special between them. And what was that something? Physical attraction. And what was wrong with that? Nothing. Getting involved with a man did not necessarily mean a serious commitment and marriage. Most often it did not mean that.

She did not want to get married. She did not want to give up her precious freedom. Not again, not ever. Not for any amount of money. But that didn't mean that she couldn't have a relationship.

Over a cup of cappuccino, she discussed it with her savvy friend, Carol, who'd come down to pay her a visit. Carol had had more experience with men than she had—two long affairs with serious lovers, one short marriage to a nonserious husband and many casual outings with casual men. Right now she was unattached and not enjoying it. Christina didn't think this state of affairs would last long. Carol was striking rather than beautiful. Her straight black hair cut stylishly short made her look a bit French. She had luminous green eyes and a slim body unravaged by pregnancy and childbirth.

"So this guy is drop-dead gorgeous, rich, sexy, charming, dynamic, and he wants you," Carol enumerated in a businesslike tone.

Christina nodded. "Yes. Tell me what's wrong with that."

"Everything," Carol said promptly, crossing her long, shapely legs at the ankles.

Christina sighed. "Why?" she asked feebly.

"Rich, handsome, sexy, charming men are not to be trusted. They've got monumental egos and selfish agendas."

Christina made a face. "I was afraid you'd say that."

Carol arched a perfectly shaped eyebrow. "What did you want me to say?"

"To go for it and enjoy myself."

Carol laughed. "You can still do that. Just don't trust him."

"You can't have an honest relationship that way."

Carol picked up her coffee cup and gave a light shrug. "You can have a good time for a while. Just don't imagine a grand passion, eternal love, marriage, all that stuff.''

''I don't want to get married.''

''I know. You've said that once or twice.'' Carol's voice was dry. ''So what is the problem?''

''I don't know, really. I guess I'm scared.''

''Of what?''

Christina looked gloomily into her empty cup, where the remainder of the frothy milk now looked brown and scummy. ''Of losing my mind and messing up my life.''

''Well, that would be serious.'' Carol frowned and ran her fingers through her short cap of black hair. ''Okay, tell me the worst-case scenario. What is the worst thing that could happen?''

Christina felt her stomach begin to churn. She took a deep breath. ''Okay. The worst thing that could happen is that I would fall seriously in love with him and he with me, after which he would ask me to marry him and I would be foolish enough to say yes because I am blind and stupid and then after we're married for a while he'd get enough of me and my stretch marks and find some blond bimbo half my age with big breasts and a flat stomach and out I'd go.''

''Ouch.'' Carol looked pained. ''History repeating itself, so to speak.''

Christina nodded. ''Yes.''

''Well, just remember that whatever you do, don't marry the man.''

Christina nodded. ''And who says he'll ever ask me in the first place? I'm just overreacting.''

What she should do was lighten up and not act like a frightened virgin. They could just get to know each other and enjoy each other. There was nothing wrong with that, was there? They were both mature people who could have a mature relationship without getting all tangled up in the emotional morass of love and commitment.

She took a deep breath. She was an independent, sophisticated woman; surely she could handle a mature relationship with Jack Millard?

One week later, she was not sure she could handle it at all, maturely or otherwise. She was doing battle with her heart, her emotions and her sanity and knew she was losing. Falling head over heels in love was not what a mature woman of forty-two ought to allow herself to do. It was so juvenile! It was so dangerous!

She talked to Jack on the phone every day, and he came to the inn to spend time with her on Tuesday and Wednesday, her days off.

He told her crazy tales of his adventures around the world, making her laugh. They took long walks in the woods and talked about children, about work, about traveling—ordinary things that suddenly seemed fascinating.

They had many things in common, including the love of food and travel, and the fact that they each had a foreign grandparent. Christina had a very proper English grandmother who had taught her the joys of afternoon tea. Jack had an eccentric French grandmother who had encouraged in him his lust for rebellion.

There were differences, too. Christina, as a child, had been a good girl who did what was expected of her and never caused her parents a moment of worry. Jack had been distinctly on the wild side, skipping school routinely because there was a whole world out there begging to be explored. His parents had worried a lot.

They'd given up worrying now, although Jack hadn't stopped doing wild things, such as creating the "Garbage Department" at the family company headquarters.

Getting to know Jack was like unearthing a marvelous treasure little by little, day by day. Jack Millard was special. Christina discovered that beneath his teasing, fun-loving ways, he had a solid core. She liked it. She liked his wicked smile, his seducing eyes, the woodsy scent of his after-shave, the way he talked about his kids.

He kissed her, saying she had lovely, sensuous lips, stroked her softly, intimately, but did not take her to bed to make love, as if he wanted to give her time, thought she needed it.

She'd thought she needed time, too, but she was beginning to change her mind fast.

"Have you slept with him yet?" Carol asked over the phone one afternoon. "Was he any good?"

"Carol!"

A chuckle bubbled over the phone line. "Am I being too indiscreet?"

"Yes. And the answer is no, I haven't."

"What's keeping you?"

"For heaven's sake, it's only been a few days! We're not bunny rabbits!"

"They have a lot of fun, I hear. So what are you doing? Having intellectual discussions about politics and quantum physics, repressing all those lovely carnal desires? Sounds unhealthy to me."

"Oh, be quiet, Carol!"

Carol laughed. "Don't forget, at your age you only have a few decades left, so if I were you I'd cram in the physical pleasures as soon and as often as I could, but—"

"Oh, stop it, Carol!" Christina said, cutting her off. "I've got to run. Talk to you later."

Her calm, quiet existence seemed to have turned upside down and inside out. Although her daily routine remained the same, it felt as if she had walked through some magical door and everything was different, more beautiful, more special. The sky had never been bluer, the rain never more refreshing. She felt dizzy, as restless as a leaf fluttering in the breeze, light on her feet like a dancer. Dancing.

Her heart danced when she heard his voice over the phone, danced as he took her hand in his own warm, big one. When he kissed her good-night, it would dance frantically.

She didn't feel very sophisticated in her reactions. She felt mesmerized, possessed, and she tried to hide it with all her might. She didn't want to look like a silly schoolgirl hopelessly in love.

She *was* hopelessly in love. At forty-two. She, the mother of a grown daughter.

A grown daughter who came home for the weekend, took one look at her face and grinned broadly.

"Bowled you over good, didn't he?" she stated with obvious glee.

"What are you talking about?" Christina asked, pretending ignorance.

"Jack Millard," Dana said patiently. "Gorgeous, sexy, exciting Jack Millard managed to sweep you off your feet. I knew he could do it."

For some reason, Christina felt almost embarrassed. "He didn't sweep me off my feet," she lied. "We're seeing each other, that's all."

Dana's blue eyes sparkled with amusement. She leaned closer toward her. "Mom," she whispered, "you're lying." Then she broke out in laughter. "This is cool! This is so cool!"

Christina was at work in her office when Jack unexpectedly appeared in front of her desk. Her heart made a delighted leap in her chest. He was wearing a suit and tie and an unbuttoned Burberry coat, all sophisticated male appeal, except for his hair, which the wind had blown into disarray, adding a rakish sexiness. She stifled the delicious urge to run her fingers through it to smooth it out.

"Hi," she said, looking at his grinning face.

"Hi." He leaned across her desk and planted a kiss on her mouth, apparently not caring who might pass by the open door and see him. One thing she loved so much about him was his lack of concern for the opinion of others. "I know I am severely disturbing you," he said, "and I sincerely hope you don't mind."

"I don't mind," she said like a woman hopelessly in love, which she was. Her heart was making joyful little somersaults. He was disturbing her all right. Every little inch of her. She took a deep breath. "I thought you'd be working today," she said.

"I wanted to see you and work will wait." He walked around the desk, took her hand and pulled her out of her chair. "Let's go for a walk. There's something I want to talk to you about."

She gave him a searching look. "All right." She took her coat, wrapped a scarf around her neck and pulled on her gloves. It was windy and cold outside.

She braced herself against the frigid temperature as they stepped outside. Jack pulled up the collar of his coat as he glanced up at the sky. It had the color of lead. "How about a trip to a tropical paradise?" he asked. "You and me in the warm, warm sun."

"Sounds good to me," she said, shivering.

He put his arm around her, drawing her close to his side as they strolled down the uneven path. "Great! Let's do it. Pack your bags. We'll leave on Monday."

"You're nuts, Jack," she said mildly.

"You're not the first to say that, but it works for me." He grinned devilishly. "Live a little. Pack your suitcase and I'll sweep you off to paradise. I think it's high time for you to be swept away."

He was serious. She couldn't believe it. It was ridiculous! She looked into his smiling face. "Pack my bags and go away with you? Just like that? You're crazy, Jack!" Responsible people didn't do this sort of thing. *She* didn't do this sort of thing.

They'd stopped walking and stood facing each other. Jack put his hands on her shoulders.

"Ah, but a little craziness is so much fun, Christina. Try it. Live a little. Be a little wild. Go for the adventure. Isn't that what you secretly long for?"

"That doesn't mean I'd actually *do* it! I can't!" She gave him a suspicious look. "What are you cooking up, Jack? What brought this on?"

"I'm not cooking up anything, but I think maybe the gods are." His voice was dry.

"The gods?"

He nodded gravely. "Something odd happened, and I don't think it was a coincidence."

CHAPTER SEVEN

CHRISTINA shivered in the cold and pushed her hands into her pockets. "Something odd? What?"

He dropped his hands from her shoulders and they started walking again toward the woods, which looked gray and somber in their winter nakedness. "An old friend called me early this morning," Jack said. "I hadn't seen or talked to him for over a year."

"Sometimes that happens," she said, failing to see why that should be odd.

"It wasn't just that. He has a business venture he'd like me to invest in. He invited me to come to his house and stay for a few days next week and discuss the project, and he said to bring you along if I wanted to and make a little vacation out of it." He smiled. "And I want to."

"He knows about me?"

"I told him about you."

"I see." She frowned. "That's nice, of course, but why is that odd?"

He looked straight into her eyes. "He and his wife Teresa, live on a tiny island in the Caribbean. St. Barlow."

She felt a prickling of recognition. "An island in the Caribbean?" she repeated.

He nodded. "Blue skies, white beaches, palm trees. They have a white house on the beach. The center of the island is mountainous, covered with rain forest. It's a beautiful place."

She stared at him, memory flooding back. The mind-travel game he'd played with her the night of the storm.

107

She swallowed. "And you know I'll just love it," she said slowly.

"Yes."

She nodded. "You're right, it's odd." She hesitated, which didn't escape him.

"I know what you're thinking. Go ahead, say it," he urged.

"Unless it's not odd at all, and that invitation from your friend did not just come falling out of the sky."

"Right. Only I don't lie, Christina. Which is not to say that I would not have been capable of orchestrating an event of this nature. I would have, and I might have, but I didn't."

She believed him. Any woman in love would have, of course, which was not a reassuring thought. She wanted to believe she was more intelligent, more savvy than those foolish types who ended up on the talk shows saying what happened to them could happen to anybody. She didn't want to think she was just anybody.

"I'd like you to come with me," he said. "Monday to Thursday next week." He sat down on a weathered wooden bench, stretching out his legs. "It will be a good opportunity to spend some time together."

Longing stirred, a crazy, dangerous longing to break away and do something wild and crazy, to be away from the daily routine.

To be alone with Jack.

He reached for her hand and pulled her down next to him. "I'm having visions of your seducing me on a moonlit beach one night."

She gaped at him, taken aback by his words.

He laughed. "Alternatively, I can seduce you, if you prefer." He put his arms around her. "I'm trying not to pressure you, but I have to admit I'm not much of a saint. I want to make love to you."

She sucked in a breath of cold air. "You don't have to carry me off to some obscure island to make love to me."

"No. I could do it right here, on this bench, or in your office or cabin, but I have a weakness for romance. I want it to be special. This island is a special place. It's romantic and magical and beautiful. And I want us to make romantic, magical and beautiful love together."

Her face lay against his shoulder and she absorbed his words, thinking how nice it was that he wanted it to be special, that being on an island would be so romantic. Her magazines were full of pictures of tropical islands, so pure, so idyllic. And moonlight was good, came the fleeting thought, soft and not too revealing.

There are no coincidences, Dana had said. *Everything happens for a reason.* Her imagination had conjured up a tropical island, generic as the vision might have been. Now there was a sudden chance to go to just such a place. Was it more than just coincidence?

It was more interesting to think that the gods had cooked up something. Destiny. A person couldn't fight destiny, so perhaps she shouldn't try. Fate had offered her an opportunity and she should accept it.

There were a thousand reasons and excuses why she shouldn't go, including the fact that she had a business to run, but with a courage she didn't know she possessed, she swept them aside. Carl, she knew, would be more than happy to run the kitchen by himself.

Jack drew away a little and looked into her face. "Come with me," he ordered. "Live dangerously."

Live dangerously. It sounded so exciting!

"I'd love to come with you," she said bravely. Never before in her life had she felt so reckless. It was terrifying; it was exhilarating. She felt her heart pump, felt the adrenaline rush through her.

Jack stared at her, stunned for a moment. Then his face broke out in a smile that lit up his eyes as if he was delighted by a special gift. "Really?"

She chuckled. "You look surprised."

"I thought you'd come up with all kinds of reasons not to be able to do it."

"I have all kinds of reasons why I shouldn't or can't do it, but the hell with them," she said with a sweep of her arm. She had an odd sense of freedom, of pushing back invisible boundaries, of throwing off shackles.

His laugh was warm and rich, and he hugged her tightly against him. "You've got guts. I like that." He kissed her forehead. "And a sense of adventure, and I like that, too." He kissed her nose. "All around, you are a very special woman."

She leaned into him. There were too many layers of clothes between them. Heavy jackets, thick sweaters. She longed to hear his heart. She longed to get rid of all those clothes. She longed to feel warm sunshine on her skin, a fresh breeze stirring her hair, clear turquoise waters swirling around her ankles. She longed to be closer to him. She longed for all of him.

The panic came later. The Caribbean. Oh, God, the beach! That meant a swimsuit. She'd have to get a new one, one that held her belly in and her breasts up. What a nightmare!

She drove to Philadelphia the next morning, and with Carol along for fashion advice and moral support, she went in search of the swimsuit. She found one that held her belly in and her breasts up. It cost a fortune.

"You look great!" said Carol, who wouldn't hesitate to tell the truth if Christina looked like a sack of potatoes. "It shows off your legs and your waist. I can't imagine why you're so worried. I suppose you've still got Peter in your head telling you you're not perfect."

"I *am* not perfect."

Carol rolled her eyes. "And this Jack Millard of yours is perfect, of course."

"Yes," said Christina. He was devastatingly sexy, he was kind, he was funny, he made her body go crazy with longing. He wasn't pressuring her to sleep with him. He was trying to be considerate, even if he was having trouble with sainthood. Well, it was time for the end of sainthood; she couldn't stand it any longer.

Carol groaned. "Oh, please, do me a favor. The man camped out in a storm on your property. He has a screw loose."

"He has a great sense of humor." She gave Carol a challenging look. "He wanted to see me. I thought it was a very romantic gesture." She couldn't believe herself. She hadn't thought it a romantic gesture at all. She'd wanted to send the police after him. Amazing how your mood and emotions changed your perceptions.

Carol frowned. "You're crazy to go on a trip with this man. You hardly know him! He could be a con man!"

"You're just jealous."

Carol widened her eyes and arched her brows. "Me? Jealous? Because you're going to some tropical island with a rich, sexy guy who's going to wine and dine you and no doubt ravish you under the stars on a deserted beach?

For a fraction of a moment, the image of herself and Jack, naked on a moonlit beach, flashed before her eyes. It nearly made her heart stop.

"Yes."

Carol let her face collapse. "Okay, I'm jealous. But he could still be a çon man and I'm concerned about you taking off with him to a tiny island that isn't even on the map. I looked, you know."

"He's not a con man. The police checked him out once. I've been to his house, slept under his roof if not in his bed. I've met his kids.'' She shrugged. ''Besides, what would he con out of me? I have no money to speak of and he could find sex with somebody young and gorgeous for the price of a glass of wine or probably less.''

''So if it isn't for money or sex, why is he taking you all the way to a tropical island?''

Christina sighed. ''I keep asking myself that.''

''Maybe he's setting you up,'' Carol intoned darkly. ''Using you to do his dirty work. Drug smuggling, gun running, or something else dastardly illegal and immoral.''

''Carol!'' Her voice was a groan of despair, not of shock. After all, she'd imagined similar scenarios not so long ago.

Carol laughed. ''Then again, it might just be that he likes you for what you are, wrinkles and all. It *is* within the realm of possibility.''

''Thank you,'' Christina said dryly. ''I feel so much better now.''

''Maybe he's one of those rare men who are truly interested in a woman because of her character and personality, rather than her body.''

Christina grimaced as she began pulling off the suit. ''Wait till he sees my stretch marks.''

Carol laughed. ''Oh, God, you're scared to death, aren't you?''

''I'm terrified.''

Carol's face softened. ''Peter was such a jerk to make you feel so inadequate. Don't let that ruin things for you.''

''I'm trying. That's why I'm going to spend a king's ransom buying this damned suit.'' She squinted as she tried to read the price tag again, just to be sure she'd read the price right the first time.

''You need reading glasses, girl,'' Carol commented.

Christina glared at her. "Be quiet. This is not what I need to hear right now." She did need glasses, she knew, but she had tried to ignore this one additional indication of her ever-advancing old age. She pulled on her clothes. "Let's get out of here before I have an anxiety attack."

Monday dawned cold, wet and miserable, the landscape dreary and damp, the hills swimming in a chilling mist. All of it was mercifully left behind as Christina and Jack boarded the private jet that would fly them to St. Thomas. From there a small puddle jumper would take them to St. Barlow, whose airstrip wasn't large enough to accommodate the jet. It was like entering another universe.

Ah, such luxury! The plane was warm and bright, with fresh flowers and a smiling attendant with Bambi eyes ready to fulfill her every wish as if she were royalty.

She was impressed, of course. How could she not be? Such extravagance to have a plane all to yourself! It was quite unbelievable. Jack was sitting next to her in the wide, comfortable seat, legs stretched out in front of him, his face amused as he watched her.

Christina felt as if she were in a romantic movie, sitting next to this stunningly sexy man, on her way to a tropical island for a few days of indulgence and temptation. Oh boy, how had this ever happened to her?

Lunch was served almost immediately, accompanied by a bottle of chilled Dom Pérignon.

"It's only barely afternoon," she protested, but not too loudly.

He grinned. "So what? Champagne is for celebrations and I don't care what time it is."

"Is this a celebration?"

He grinned. "You bet. I've got you up in the clouds, captive at twenty-some thousand feet above Mother Earth. I'm a lucky man." His eyes were full of devilish delight and it was hard not to smile. He raised his glass to hers. "To living dangerously."

Lunch was delicious. After a couple of glasses of champagne, she was decidedly mellow. "I feel quite decadent," she said. "And spoiled and indulged. Actually, it's almost like being in a fantasy."

"Fantasies are good." His mouth teased her earlobe. "But just sitting here with me drinking champagne is rather a bland fantasy. Let's spice it up a bit."

"You'd want me to take off my clothes, I imagine," she said mockingly. Bambi had cleared their dishes and disappeared in the front of the plane.

"That would certainly make it more interesting."

"You can forget it. I've had two glasses of champagne, but it would take a lot more than that for me to even consider it."

"Like what?"

"Like a gun to my head."

He threw his head back and laughed.

"And even then," she went on, "I might consider dying with my clothes on a more respectable alternative."

He looked wounded. "More acceptable than making passionate love with me in the clouds?"

He did have a way with words. How poetic he sounded! Making love in the clouds, floating in ecstasy—such heavenly delights! Oh, sure.

She thought of the possibility of lusty romps in the plane seat, of the captain coming to say hello, or Bambi returning to see if they were in need of more caviar or champagne, or perhaps oysters on the half shell. They'd see her naked or seminaked, in all her forty-two-year-old glory. She nearly died just thinking about it.

"Yes," she said. "And if you're looking for a woman who's kinky and wild, I'm not it."

He squeezed her hand, his eyes laughing. "I don't think you know your own potential."

She pulled her hand free. "I do know that there's no way in hell I'll fool around in a plane seat! Ever!"

"Well, good," he said soothingly. "I always knew you had class." Then he laughed. "I'm only teasing you, Christina. We were merely talking about fantasies, not my actual wishes and expectations." He picked up the bottle. "Have another glass of champagne, and I promise I won't seduce you here on board."

"You wouldn't be able to," she muttered darkly, taking a big swig of the sparkling wine.

Wisely, he did not react to that. He merely smiled, a smile so full of wicked seduction, it made her limbs feel weak.

A demitasse of espresso revived her somewhat, but the gleam in his eyes was there for the rest of the afternoon, and the warm touch of his hand promised adventure.

On St. Thomas, a lightplane was already waiting for them. After the luxury of the jet, the tiny aircraft felt like a rickety old bus, which inspired no great confidence. As they reared, rattling and shuddering into the sky, Christina had visions of crashing down into the warm waters of the tropical sea below. Well, she'd heard of worse ways to go.

Her visions, fortunately, were not transformed into reality, and she soon forgot her fears as she took in the magnificent vista of blue waters and green islands below.

St. Barlow, when it finally came into view, was a small spot of lush, verdant mountains and white sand beaches floating in a crystalline aquamarine sea.

They were met by Joe, Jack's friend, who ushered them into a bright red mini-moke, a little box of a car without a roof and sides.

It was a beautiful ride along the winding coastal road, with forested mountains reaching up to an azure sky on the right and calm turquoise waters glimmering in the late-afternoon sun on the left. Christina drank in the sights, leaving the conversation to the men, thinking that this truly was a magnificent place. She glanced at Jack, feeling a joyous excitement. Six weeks ago, she had not known this man. And now, here she was on a tropical island with him, hopelessly in love. It was a miracle.

"I'm so glad you could come along," Teresa said as she showed Christina to her room.

She was about Christina's age, had curly auburn hair and warm brown eyes. The colorful, jungle-print dress she wore gave her generous form a cheerful, casual appearance. Her smile was open and friendly.

"I hope this room is all right. Jack's is right next door, and you share the veranda." She hesitated for a moment, a spark of humor in her eyes. "We weren't sure if you wanted to share a room, although I thought you probably would, the way Jack talked about you on the phone, but I didn't want to be wrong. Anyway, feel free to do as you please." She went to open the slatted doors leading onto the veranda, relieving Christina of having to make a reply.

There was a magical view of the mountains with the sun setting behind them streaking the sky in a splendor of color. Christina looked at it in awe.

"This is wonderful," she said, smiling at Teresa. "Thank you for inviting me to come."

"We're happy to have you, and to be honest, I was happy to hear Jack had found himself another woman. I wondered if he ever would, you know."

"Why?"

"Well, Sara was a very special person, and he loved her and they were so happy together. When she died, he was devastated."

Christina felt her stomach twisting, felt a sudden sense of dread. What Teresa was telling her was not news to her. Jack himself had said he'd loved his wife and that they'd been happy. Why should that bother her? Shame on her. It was a wonderful thing, marital love, not that she knew anything about it, but that's what she'd heard.

"We want him to be happy again," Teresa went on. "We'd love to see him remarried." Teresa smiled. "He's a wonderful man."

Married. Christina didn't know why the breath suddenly caught in her throat, why she suddenly felt an odd sense of panic. Married. She swallowed, struggling for composure.

"Did you know her?" she asked. "His wife, I mean."

"Sara?" Teresa nodded. "We were friends." She gave Christina a searching look. "I blew it, didn't I? Not very sensitive of me to bring her up."

Christina forced herself to smile. "Sara is no secret. Of course we can talk about her. I saw her photographs at Jack's house, the ones she took of the children. She was very talented."

Relief suffused Teresa's face. "Yes, she was." She glanced around the room in an obvious effort to find something to change the subject. "If you need anything, just let me know," she said, moving to the door.

"Thank you. Everything looks wonderful," Christina said truthfully.

"Why don't you get yourself settled and then come down to the terrace for sundowners? It's out through the living room."

Christina nodded. "Thanks, I will." A drink at this point seemed like a good idea. Maybe even two. She was here to relax, not to get her stomach twisted into a knot about the long-departed Sara.

Teresa left and Christina glanced around the room in delight, taking in the rattan furniture, the huge, comfortable bed, the view of the mountains. The wooden shutters were open and a trade-wind breeze wafted into the room carrying the scents of sea and tropical flowers.

The bathroom was luxurious in white and soft sea green. She was dying to get out of her winter clothes and pull on something light and airy. And why not? She had a quick shower and dressed in a simple long dress, sleeveless and cool, in various muted shades of raspberry pink. She put on long, dangling earrings and high-heeled sandals and glanced at herself in the mirror. She looked summery and fresh. A few dabs of a flowery fragrance in strategic places and she was ready. But first she'd check out the view from the veranda.

As she stepped out through the open slatted doors, Jack emerged from his room next door, dressed in white chinos and a blue silk shirt, looking relaxed and fit. She felt her pulse leap. She wanted to throw her arms around him, but checked the impulse. She'd checked similar impulses a lot, feeling a little awkward with all that blossoming need for closeness and intimacy.

"It's so beautiful," she said instead, and he smiled.

"So are you," he said, putting his arms around her, he, who had no difficulty expressing his need for closeness and intimacy. "Mmm, you smell nice."

He did, too—of soap and after-shave, very manly, very sexy. His hair was damp. She felt his body warmth through the thin silk shirt, felt a warmth of her own flooding through her, felt a restless need, a longing.

Lust, she thought. Plain and simple. She should be so happy not to be sexually dead.

"How is your room?" he asked.

"It's wonderful. And yours?"

"Lonely," he said. "I want you in it with me."

Her heart turned over. She swallowed, feeling his hand stroking her hair, trailing down her back. Feeling her breasts swell against his chest.

"I want to look at you and touch you and kiss you and make love to you," he said, his tone growing low and husky. "And I want to go to sleep with you in my arms, and when I wake up I want you to be right there with me in the bed."

The images his words created stirred in her a rush of desire. She felt his hands softly cup her breasts, felt their warmth through the thin fabric of her dress and bra. He was looking into her eyes with a dark hunger that made the air lodge in her chest. She couldn't tear her gaze away and she stood there breathless and transfixed, his hands on her breasts. He slipped his hands back around her shoulders and lowered his mouth on hers, kissing her with blatant sexual desire. Heat raced like wildfire through every inch and cell of her body.

"Stay with me tonight," he whispered against her lips, his breath warm, his body hot and close against hers. "Let's make love, you and I."

"Yes," she whispered back, and there was no thought, no reasoning, just the knowledge that she wanted him and needed him.

He released her reluctantly and gave her a smile that glimmered darkly in his eyes. "Only problem is we're expected on the terrace for drinks and then we'll have to make it through dinner. You think we can manage it?"

They managed it, but it wasn't easy.

Yet it was an interesting evening, with good conversation and wonderful food she'd never eaten before—grilled parrot fish and breadfruit fritters and fresh mango ice cream for dessert. But Christina felt as if she were only half there, as if she were merely going through the motions. All she could think of was later, of being alone with Jack, of taking her clothes off, of Jack taking his clothes off. And while she was thinking all those wild and secret thoughts, she had to act like a calm, rational person making calm, rational conversation, eating dinner. It was not the sort of challenge she was used to.

Making love was something else she wasn't used to. She hadn't been with a man for years, and her experiences with her worthless husband did not make her feel inspired or confident. Tonight it was going to happen and she yearned for it and feared it at the same time. What if she made a fool of herself? What if she really wasn't any good at it?

That could be a topic of another talk show.

The evening seemed to last an eternity. But it was just after eleven when they wished their hosts good-night.

Jack took her hand and drew her into his room and closed the door with a kick of his foot. There was something firm and final about the sound of the door closing behind them and she felt a nervous shiver go down her back.

The room was lit by a small bedside lamp, which he must have left on before going to dinner. The louvered doors leading to the terrace stood open, letting in the cool evening breeze. The moon glimmered through the waving palm fronds. Jack looked so big in this small room—big and overpowering and so very male. Her stomach tightened and her heart seemed to stumble over itself.

Reaching up, Jack trailed his fingers through her hair, softly, seductively. She stood very still, barely breathing. He cradled her face, smiling down at her. His eyes were full of dark fire and she felt herself begin to tremble, knowing what was coming—wanting it, fearing it.

CHAPTER EIGHT

"You're trembling," he said quietly.

She swallowed. "I'm nervous and it makes me feel silly to feel that way."

He laughed softly. "There's nothing to be nervous about. Just let it happen."

She closed her eyes, feeling his hands warm on her cheeks. "I want to."

She wanted to just let it happen. She wanted not to worry about it anymore—about what he might think about her body, about not measuring up, about making a fool of herself. She wanted to feel open and eager, to be free of fear and worry. She wanted to let go and allow herself to feel all the passion and urgency and desire leashed inside her.

His hands slipped away from her face and he unbuttoned his shirt, stripped it off and tossed it on a chair. Her gaze took in his solid chest, sprinkled with dark hair, the kind of strong, comforting chest you wanted to put your cheek against—to feel safe and loved. A hunger, intense and deep, welled up inside her. She took in a slow, long breath.

It wasn't the first time she'd seen his bare chest; she'd seen it as he was sitting in the tub in the Snuggery the day he had come to the inn, filthy and dangerous-looking. He didn't look dangerous now. He looked . . . exciting, vital, virile. He reached around her and slowly unzipped her dress, allowing it to pool at her feet, leaving her with nothing on but her bra and panties—brand-new ones, lacy and pretty and very expensive. She'd felt deliciously extravagant buying them, and also a little silly. Still, she liked the way the delicate things looked on her, and after all, she wasn't ancient yet. She could wear sexy lingerie if she wanted to.

She took in a ragged breath. In a moment he was going to take off her bra. Her heart was racing. She didn't want him to see her totally naked; she wanted the blasted light off. It would be easier if he couldn't see too much of her.

He teased her mouth as he reached for the back closure of her bra. She squirmed away from his warm fingers.

"Please," she whispered, "let's turn off the light."

"I want to see you."

"Please, just turn it off."

He reached over and did as she asked. "Why can't I see you?" His lips brushed seductively across hers, then trailed down her throat.

"Because it embarrasses me." She swallowed. "I'm not exactly twenty anymore."

He laughed. "You sure fooled me."

"Don't make fun of me."

"May I remind you that I am not twenty anymore, either?" His mouth was warm against the top of her breasts, just above the lace of her bra.

"It's different for men. They look better as they get older, more distinguished, more...interesting and attractive."

"Sounds sexist to me."

"It's the truth, in people's minds, at any rate."

"Forget what's in people's minds." He trailed damp kisses back up her throat to her cheek and temple. "In my mind, you are beautiful and desirable and I thought that the first time I saw you." His mouth was warm against her ear. "You're a loving, wonderful, sexy woman and I've wanted you for a long time and nothing is going to change that, certainly not a bedroom lamp."

He was too good to be true. She sighed. "I'm sorry I'm such a...I don't know what. I suppose you'd rather—"

He silenced her with his mouth, unhooking her bra at the same time and tossing it aside. He cupped her breasts, his hands gentle on her skin. "You're soft and warm and lovely," he whispered.

Her heart beat erratically, and all she could do was stand there as his hands stroked their way down her waist and hips, slipping off her panties. He picked her up and lowered her to the bed before taking off the rest of his own clothes.

She watched him in the shadowy moonlight filtering through the palm trees, spilling into the room. His lean, powerful frame moved easily and quickly and he was next to her on the bed only moments later—next to her, not touching. He smiled down at her, his face close, and she felt exposed and vulnerable under his regard.

She felt the heat of him radiating onto her skin, felt the sexual energy reaching out to her, enveloping her, filling her. "Just relax," he whispered, and began to caress her body, only his hands touching her. He stroked her belly, the curve of her hip. "I like how you feel—very soft, very womanly." His voice was low, the words like a caress, feathering her senses. She drank in the sound and felt the rich blooming of desire. Then his mouth joined his hands in the pleasuring, kissing her breasts, teasing her nipples with his tongue. Her breath caught in her throat at the exquisite, tingling sensation rippling all through her. It felt so good, so good.

His mouth and hands made magic everywhere on her body. She let out a soft sigh, all thought swept away by the swirling of dizzy desire in her blood and the need to touch him, to feel him.

A need so overwhelming and mindless, it made her head reel. And then came the flash of awareness of what was happening, of the glorious knowing her body was whole and lush and throbbing with life and passion, of knowing she wanted this man with all her being. She reached out to him, pressing herself against him, skin against skin, hot and eager. She gave a low moan and found his mouth, kissing him with a drunken urgency.

The kiss was like an explosion, obliterating all thought, all sense of time and place. Fire. Heat.

A dance of rapture, her blood singing, her body moving to ancient rhythms, a swirling of color and light. Such aching sweetness, such delicious agony.

"Christina…" His voice was a husky whisper. He drew away slightly, gazing into her eyes, his breath fast and shallow. His body was rigid with tension.

She saw the raw hunger, the passion, but tenderness, as well. He stroked a damp tendril of hair away from her face, the gesture caring and sweet and her heart flowed over.

"I wanted to make this last," he said a little breathlessly, his mouth slanting in humor. "But it's not going to."

"No," she murmured, feeling her body throb and ache. "It's not." She touched his face, damp and warm under her hand. "I want you so much, it hurts," she said on a low note. "I didn't know I could want so much, feel so much."

He gave a low groan, lowering his mouth against hers, moving inside her. She felt full. Full of him, full of love and turbulent, feverish desire.

"Oh," she whimpered. "Oh, oh…" She let it happen. She let the storm sweep her along with him as they clung together and soared into bliss, tumbled into trembling release.

They lay tangled together on the rumpled sheets, replete, exhausted. She had never felt more fulfilled, more happy.

*   *   *

The few days on St. Barlow were magic. They hiked in the rain forest and made love by a waterfall. They slept on the beach and made love under the stars. The lushness of the island, the verdant, exotic greenery, added to her feeling of being exquisitcly alive—a sense of blooming and flowering like the luxuriant vegetation around her. The place had a mesmerizing effect on her, making her feel as if she had been transported to another dimension. Spending the nights curled up in Jack's arms, sleeping or making love, had a lot to do with this sensation of being in a different dimension. A magical dimension indeed. He made music with her body, making her feel beautiful and joyously alive.

Friday morning she awoke, feeling a little sad. Today they would leave, and she didn't want to. She'd cheerfully stay another week, another month. Let Carl take care of the inn.

Propped up on his elbow, chin resting in his hand, Jack was looking down at her with a faint smile. "If we were married, we could do this every day," he said casually.

Married. Stunned for a moment, she could only stare at him. Then panic assailed her. Marriage. She didn't want marriage. She'd lose her freedom and independence. A wave of old pain and new fear washed over her. Her hands were suddenly damp and her heart was racing as if her body was gearing up to hightail it out of the room, out of the house and off the island.

He was watching her, waiting for a response. She needed to say something, anything. It took an effort to keep her composure and feign nonchalance.

"We'd just start taking it for granted," she said, trying desperately to inject her voice with some lightness. Her smile was stiff. She slipped out of bed before he could reach her and detain her. Slipping on her robe, she went out through the slatted wooden doors and stood on the veranda, her heart beating too fast, her mouth dry as dust. The mountains swam in a silvery sheen of morning mist that would soon burn off. The world gleamed with new light, new promises. Birds warbled and chirped in joyous celebration.

Her stomach churned. Her body felt clammy as if she were going to be sick. This was crazy, crazy. She took in a deep breath of the fragrant air, feeling the cool breeze stroke her warm face.

He was standing beside her. "What's wrong?" he asked, his voice calm. "You took off like a rocket."

She took in another deep breath, trying again for a touch of lightness. "I seem to have an allergic reaction to the subject of marriage. I think I told you once I . . . I don't want to be married again."

He sighed. "I forgot. I just got carried away. It was a nice fantasy there for a very short, sweet moment. Eating dinner with you every night, sleeping with you every night, making love whenever we felt like it. Just having you part of my life all the time." His mouth quirked. "Such foolish dreams."

"It's better this way," she said soothingly, amazed at her own presence of mind. "If we were married, you'd get tired of me really quickly. I'm not good wife material, so to speak." Not for a man like Jack, who had a world of options and opportunities, not to speak of temptations.

He frowned at her, his eyes suddenly dark with anger. In the cool morning stillness, voices drifted toward the terrace. Teresa, talking to the gardener. Jack took Christina's hand and drew her back into the room.

"You don't have much of an opinion of yourself, do you? You still have that louse of a husband lurking around in your consciousness, wreaking havoc." He sounded exasperated.

She stiffened in defense, at the same time surprised by his choice of words. They hadn't often talked about Peter, and her miserable marriage was hardly a subject she relished discussing while having a good time with Jack.

"Leave Peter out of it," she snapped, pulling her hand free.

"Only if you will." Jack glowered at her. "Get rid of him, Christina. Stop defining yourself by his twisted standards. You're a lovely, sexy, desirable woman, apart from being talented and competent, as well. Any *real* man would be happy to have you for his wife."

She was rendered speechless, her mind floundering like a drunken clown. She'd been poised to lash back at him, but his words had paralyzed the urge completely.

"Well, thank you," she managed finally, not knowing how she could be angry with him in the face of such a lovely compliment. "But I think I'd rather be free just the same." It was a lot safer that way.

"Who says you can't be free while you're married? It's time to forget the past, Christina, and forge a new life for yourself. Be courageous. Be daring."

She clenched her hands into fists. "I'm never getting married again."

He studied her face for a moment. "I suppose I've got myself a challenge on my hands," he said calmly.

"I'd prefer for you not to look at our relationship that way," she said tightly. "Can't we just enjoy it the way it is? Why do we have to talk about marriage? We've been together only a short time."

He studied her for a moment. "I'm going too fast for you and you're scared," he stated. He looked thoughtful. "I've always known what I wanted rather quickly and acted on it. I've never seen the use of lingering around."

"Sometimes it's good to stop and think before making major decisions," she lectured.

He nodded. "I do that. I stop and think and then I make the decision. And once I've made a decision, there's no stopping me."

"Is that a threat?"

His brows shot up. "A threat? Good heavens, woman, no." He put his arms firmly around her. "It's a statement of fact. Pure and simple."

And then he kissed her, the kind of kiss that made clear he had made up his mind about what was going to happen right then and there in that cool white room with the fragrant Caribbean breeze wafting in through the open doors and window.

And she, besotted fool that she was, let every sane thought vacate her brain, and allowed herself to be swept away by the promise of that kiss. Such a magic kiss...

Afterward, they lingered in bed, sated and lazy, not talking. She wasn't sure how long they'd simply lain there, when a thought surfaced in her fuzzy mind.

She dragged herself to a sitting position and looked at his face. His hair lay over his forehead and his eyes were closed. "I want to ask you a question," she said.

"Mmm," he muttered lazily, not stirring.

"How long did you know your wife before you married her?"

He opened his eyes, looking at her dazedly for a moment as if her question hadn't quite registered. Then he grinned. "Three months, but I asked her after one. It took me two months to convince her marriage was a good idea." His eyes locked with hers. "And it was," he added. "A very good idea."

"If it's such a good idea, why haven't you remarried before now? You've been alone for seven years." A man like Jack Millard—it was truly amazing.

He gave her a rueful little smile. "There wasn't anybody I wanted to marry." He took her hand and put it on his chest where his heart was. "There wasn't anybody who stirred my heart."

It had to be his French genes, she thought, for him to be saying something sentimental like that. Or maybe the magic of the island. And for a fleeting, dizzy moment, she wished she could banish the doubt, get rid of the ghosts of the past. Allow herself to be trusting and eager and believing, to accept with both hands what was offered.

But fear held her tightly in its grip, and hopes and dreams had no chance.

He didn't mention marriage again. They went home, and after all the tropical splendor of the island, they landed in the snow and it was time to think about Christmas. Jack invited her to come with him to several parties, which was a problem because they were mostly on weekends when she was working, but Carl insisted that he would be happy to take care of the weekends without her if he could have his wife, Gina, assist him instead. He loved cooking and he loved being in charge of the kitchen.

Christina hired Gina for the nights she would be gone, knowing she was a lucky woman to have such trust-worthy employees, knowing her business was safe in Carl's culinary hands.

She went shopping for clothes with Carol. She didn't have party clothes and she wanted to look nice. Actually, she wanted to look spectacular, which would be a challenge, she supposed.

It was a challenge. Having slipped on a sexy, slinky black dress, she looked at herself sideways in the fitting-room mirror and groaned in despair.

"I have a gut," she said in disgust.

"You do not have a gut," Carol said emphatically. "Sumo wrestlers have guts." Carol herself was very slim and had great taste in clothes.

"All right, my stomach sticks out."

"Your stomach is a little rounded. You are a *woman*. You have carried a child, given birth. Of course your stomach isn't flat like Barbie's. Do you want to look like Barbie?"

"Yes," Christina said, trying to suck in her stomach.

Carol groaned. "God, you're pathetic. Actually, I think you're becoming dangerously obsessed."

"I'm not obsessed. I'm being realistic." She let out her stomach, which act threatened to rip the side seams of the dress. She looked like an aging prostitute in this thing; it was so demoralizing.

"Being realistic means you accept the facts and live with them. And to tell you the truth, you are being *boring*, girl."

Christina gave her a withering look. "Oh, please, don't let me bore you!"

"If you think you have trouble now, wait till menopause hits. Not only could you have trouble with your body, you might also have trouble with your mind. My older sister is a raving maniac at times and drives everybody around her insane."

Christina glared at Carol's reflection in the mirror. "Oh, thank you! You're such comfort! I'm sure Jack would be delighted if he knew what he's in for if he hangs around long enough."

"Luckily, you have a few more years."

"A few more years until total destruction and insanity. What a future. I might as well just give up right now and crawl in a cave."

"You're being *boring*."

Christina sighed. "I know I am. I don't seem to be able to help myself."

"Being boring is one sure way to lose a man's interest, so get with it, girl. Smile, be bright, be sunny, make intelligent conversation. Use your mind while you still have one."

Christina groaned as she peeled off the slinky dress. "Shut up, Carol."

"You should try a dress with a long, flared skirt, something loose and sexy that kind of floats around your ankles. You've got great ankles."

Great ankles. She should be grateful for small mercies.

"Wear strappy high-heeled shoes, paint your toenails. You've got nice feet, which isn't what most women can say."

"Thank you, Carol. My breasts sag, my stomach sticks out, my hair is graying, I'm on the brink of menopause, but I have nice feet. I'm really starting to feel better. Why don't you just shoot me?"

"Too messy. Besides, Jack would be so unhappy. He wants you, defects and all. Don't be so selfish. Think about him."

"I *am* thinking about him. I'm thinking he ought to get himself someone young and sexy and gorgeous."

Carol took the dress and began hanging it back up. "Maybe you should let him decide whom he wants. He's a big boy, perfectly capable of making his own choices. And obviously he wants you, with all your many imperfections, because he sees something more important than your body. Give him a little credit, will you? And now I need to fortify myself with a double espresso before you bore me to death."

Christina had to silently admit to herself that she should be happy to have a blunt, honest friend like Carol, someone who could keep things in perspective for her. She put her clothes back on and they went in search of espresso.

In the end, of course, they found some gorgeous clothes, and Christina's insecurities made a retreat. She felt happy. In the right kind of clothes, she looked good, sexy even.

Jack, too, seemed to think so when he saw her that Friday night in the blue-and-green silk dress. She could see it in his eyes, his face, and pleasure thrilled through her. She'd come to his house that afternoon to change her clothes and get ready for the party. The dress hugged her waist, then flared softly over her hips to her ankles. The shimmering colors reminded her of the Caribbean—the crystalline sea with its many shades of aquamarine and turquoise, the azure sky. The colors brightened the blue of her eyes and made them shine. She twirled around on tiptoe and the silk swirled and swished sensuously around her ankles.

"You look . . . beautiful." His voice was as soft as a caress. A joyous warmth suffused her, making her smile, making her feel rich and euphoric.

Her smile stilled as she saw his slow intake of breath, saw the feverish darkness in his eyes. She stood still, her gaze locking with his, and something changed subtly—she felt it, sensed it. The air around them was suddenly charged with electricity—an irresistible force drawing them together. Her breath was coming in shallow little puffs as she watched him rise from the chair and come toward her. Tall and imposing in his immaculate evening clothes, he moved smoothly and easily, yet was oddly controlled. He stood in front of her, his hands softly touching her hair, sliding down her throat and bare shoulders, down to her breasts, resting there gently. Her body's reactions were instant. Warmth flooded through her like a hot tidal wave.

"We have to go to the party," she whispered.

"To hell with the party," he said huskily. He drew her to him and groaned against her mouth. "I want you.

I want you now." He kissed her with a deep, wild hunger, smearing her lipstick, messing up her hair, and she didn't care. She didn't care about anything except this wondrous mixture of love and desire that flamed through her body like wildfire. She pressed herself against him, kissing him back, feeling wanton...ravenous.

They made love right there on the silk Chinese rug—feverishly and greedily. Fast and furious. Until they collapsed against each other, breathless and trembling.

It took a long time before her heart calmed and her mind finally floated back into consciousness. She became aware that Jack was stroking her hair—so soothing after the turbulence of their lovemaking.

"I just learned something new about you," he said softly.

"I'm an animal," she muttered, vaguely embarrassed by the way they'd made love, her own shameless abandon. She'd never experienced anything so primal, so...primitive.

He chuckled. "A very sexy animal." He kissed her closed eyes. "But I was thinking of something else, something equally sexy and appealing."

"Mmm. What's that?"

He kept on stroking her tangled hair. "You just spent all kinds of time and effort to get dressed up for a party, and you didn't care one hoot about my messing it all up again."

She laughed softly. "Believe me, I know my priorities." After all, I only have a few decades left, she added silently, echoing Carol.

"I like your priorities." He sat up and grinned as he scanned her body. "You look like a woman thoroughly ravished."

She stretched lazily. "I feel thoroughly ravished."

"And you're totally unfit to go to a party in this state, as I am. We'll have to do some major restoration if we don't want people to guess what we've been doing."

"I'll run through the shower and start over."

"I'll join you." He kissed her breasts one at a time. "In a minute."

And so they showered and dressed and restored themselves.

Fortunately, her dress had not suffered any damage from having been so irreverently discarded on the floor. By the time they left the house, they looked again like civilized human beings in full control of their animal instincts.

It didn't take long after they'd arrived at the party for Christina to regret having come. They should have stayed in front of the fire and ravished each other some more. From the moment they had entered the room, women were watching the two of them with shark eyes. They mentally dissected her like a frog, cutting her to bits, scrutinizing, appraising, judging, speculating. She could see it in their faces; she wasn't stupid.

Well, this came with the territory. Jack no doubt was being drooled over by countless numbers of females. Her consolation was that he had chosen her. Because of her sparkling mind, her creativity, her intelligence... because she stirred his heart. She took a fortifying drink of champagne, and then another. The glass empty, she put it down and went in search of the ladies' room.

She heard them talking about Jack before she rounded the corner. Women's voices, three or four of them. Her breath caught in her chest, Christina froze in her high-heeled shoes. Staring blindly at a potted palm, she took in the words drifting toward her. How drop-dead handsome he was. How sexy. How rich. How fascinating. How magnificent he would be in bed. How they hadn't seen him with a woman for ages and ages.

"But he brought someone today," one of the voices said. "Did you see her?"

"She's at least *forty*. Can you believe it?"

"You say that as if it's a hundred. You'll be forty yourself soon enough, sweetheart."

"I mean, it's not what you'd *expect*. You'd think he'd come waltzing in here with some twenty-year-old sex bomb on his arm. It's not as if they're not standing in line for him."

"Including you with your Miracle Bra and your nose job."

Great hilarity. Christina sucked in a careful breath, wishing she could move, wanting to move. She stayed rooted to the spot.

"Well, I guess there's hope for me yet at the ripe old age of thirty-eight. If he's interested in her, why not in me? I'd marry him in a flash if I ever got the chance."

"Not me. And I feel sorry for her."

They were feeling sorry for her? Christina waited, rigid with an odd apprehension.

"Why are you feeling sorry for her?" The voice was incredulous.

"Just imagine her having to compete with the sainted Sara! I wouldn't even *try*! Competing with a dead wife is a lost cause, if you ask me."

"The sainted Sara?"

"He absolutely adored her, if you hear the stories. People are always saying how wonderful and sweet and talented she was. After she died, it took years before anybody saw him in public with another woman. She must have been really something." A sigh of envy and resignation followed the words.

"Still, sometimes you wonder why he fell in love with her, in the beginning, you know. I mean, it had to be hard to—"

Another group of women passed her by, laughing and talking, and the rest of the sentence was swallowed up in the noise.

It had to be hard to...what? Christina drew in a shaky breath. Her heart was throbbing, the blood pounding in her ears. The sainted Sara. Jack's wife. Paragon of all things wonderful. This was just what she needed to make her night complete. Not only did she have to watch gorgeous women lusting after him, but now she had to compete with the haunting memory of a sainted wife, as well.

Would any sane, self-respecting woman do this to herself?

Of course not. She should get out while the getting was good.

She gritted her teeth. She was sane, wasn't she?

She hoped so, but on occasion there was doubt. She was in love, madly in love, which was said to wreak havoc with your sanity. She should probably run for her life.

Instead, she walked around the corner, which stopped the conversation dead. Three women stared at her. One flaming redhead, the one she'd seen at the dinner party she had catered, one brassy blonde and one mousy brunette.

Christina smiled cheerfully. "Ladies' room that way?" she asked casually, waving down the wide marble hall.

"Yes," they said in unison.

"Thank you," she said pleasantly, and sashayed past them down the hall, feeling their collective eyes boring holes in her back.

Back in the main party room, she found Jack in search of her.

"I was looking for you," he said, putting his arm around her shoulder.

"I was circulating," she said brightly.

"Having a good time?" he asked.

She offered a brilliant smile. "Oh, yes, lovely." I'm having the time of my life, she added silently.

He gave her a narrow-eyed look. "Something wrong?"

She waved her hand casually. "It's nothing. I'd just like another glass of champagne."

"All right, let's get you one." She hadn't fooled him, of course. He'd simply decided not to pursue the conversation. What could she possibly have told him? I'm insane to be in involved with you. I'm angry and miserable because I don't want to compete with your sainted wife.

She drank the champagne a little too quickly, then had another one, which was really stupid, she knew, but she had it anyway. She smiled so much it felt as if her face was frozen in a perpetual grin.

Later, they drove to Jack's house in silence. Nicole and Matthew had gone to Vermont for the weekend, skiing with their cousins, and the house was empty and quiet.

In the living room, she sat down on the sofa, feeling a little dizzy and watched dazedly as Jack poked around in the embers and nursed a fire back to life. He looked so handsome and sexy, it brought tears to her eyes. She loved him. She knew she did. But it was hopeless, wasn't it? The champagne made her maudlin and melodramatic, she was aware, but she allowed herself to wallow in it.

"So," he said, straightening up. "What's the problem?"

He looked so tall and big and strong. He was such an exciting and vibrant man. What could he possibly see in her? How could he possibly want her, having been married to the wonderful Sara? In the end she'd only disappoint him, she knew. In the end he'd get tired of her.

Stupid tears welled up in her eyes. "I'm crazy to be involved with you," she said, saying what she didn't want to say at all. "I don't want to compete with your sainted wife."

CHAPTER NINE

His body stiffened. "My what?" he asked in a low voice.

"Your wife. The sainted Sara, they call her."

His face was like stone, his dark eyes impenetrable, and for a terrible moment he didn't say anything. "Who's they?" he demanded icily.

She shrugged. "People. Women. I hear that she was so wonderful and so special and so talented that filling her place in your life would be an almost impossible task." She swallowed. "I heard someone saying she wouldn't even try." And she was younger than I am, she almost added, but didn't. She clenched her hands in her lap and lifted her chin in outraged dignity. "And I don't want to, either!" Such drama. Oh, God, why was she saying these things? Why couldn't she shut up? What was the matter with her?

Champagne was what was the matter with her. Four glasses over the course of only a couple of hours.

He stared at her, his face dark and furious. "I don't remember asking you to fill her place in my life. I don't remember saying I *expected* you to do that."

She froze at the unfamiliar cold anger of his voice. She had never seen him so angry, and an icy wave of fear washed over her. He turned abruptly, picked up his coat and strode out of the room. She heard the front door slam.

She dragged in a ragged breath, aware she was trembling all over, that tears were streaming down her cheeks. Oh, God, what had she done? She had made him angry.

He would detest her for bringing up the name of his beloved wife.

She didn't hear the car; he must be walking. It was freezing outside and she thought of him walking the empty, lonely streets, longing for his precious Sara, wishing she had never died because nobody could take her place.

Not that he had ever said such a thing to her, of course. He had said very little about his wife, ever, except for ordinary, casual comments as they related to his past and to the children. He was a gentleman, he was.

She wished she had another glass of champagne. No, she didn't. It was the last thing she needed. If she made coffee now, she would never sleep. Besides, coffee didn't sober you up. It only woke you up.

She sat by the fire, wallowing in misery, not knowing what to do except wait for his return. *If* he returned. Maybe he would sit down on a park bench and freeze to death. Maybe he would do it on purpose so he could spend eternity with the lovely Sara. Saint Jack and Saint Sara together at last, safe in heaven, and here she was, all alone and unloved. She moaned and began to sob some more.

Then the tears dried up and she felt exhausted. She leaned her head back and closed her eyes. And somehow a measure of sanity managed to seep back into her mushy brain. She was so pathetic, sitting here awash in self-pity. She should be ashamed of herself. She, a grown woman. An independent, strong, competent woman. What possessed her to get so engulfed in sappy emotionalism?

She took another deep breath, knowing what she would have to do. She would have to be a mature person and apologize. It had been stupid to stand there and listen to what those women were saying. She shouldn't have gotten upset and said moronic things about competing with a dead person. Jack had never made her feel she had to do that, so there was no reason to feel that way just because it was suggested by some strangers with bleached hair and push-up bras.

She would make a cup of camomile tea and calm herself some more, stir up the fire and wait.

She didn't have to wait much longer.

The front door opened and closed, and moments later Jack came into the living room. "I'm sorry I walked out, but I needed time to think and to cool off," he said.

He seemed to have done the cooling-off part admirably, bringing in a tidal wave of frigid night air along with him.

"I'm sorry I made you angry," she said bravely, feeling a rush of tears behind her eyes. "I shouldn't have said what I did. I don't know what possessed me, apart from four glasses of champagne."

He moved to the fire and rubbed his hands together to warm them. His back was turned to her. "I think we need to talk about this."

She swallowed hard. "All right."

He turned to face her and she saw dark shadows in his eyes—anger, pain, she wasn't sure. He raked his hand through his hair. "Sara was my wife for fourteen years," he began. "In my opinion, she was special and wonderful, yes. I loved her, yes. And when she died I missed her more than I can tell you." He closed his eyes briefly as if it cost him an effort to speak. "But I'm not looking for anybody to fill her place. She filled her own place in my life."

He paused for a moment, his gaze meeting and holding hers. "What I want, Christina, what I need, is a woman to love and cherish and spend the rest of my life with. That does not mean I'm looking for another Sara. There is no other Sara. I loved Sara because she was uniquely herself, but that does not mean I cannot now love someone else for who she is."

Christina heard her heart pounding in the quiet that followed his words. Her tongue seemed locked in place. She didn't know what to say. He sat down next to her on the sofa, his gaze not leaving her face.

"I love you, Christina. I want to marry you. I know you're not ready for this, and that it scares you, but we'll just give it some time."

"I feel as if I'm not being fair to you." The words struggled out on a whisper. She felt guilty and scared.

"How are you not being fair to me?"

"Because I don't want to be married, and you do."

He gave a crooked little grin. "I haven't given up yet." He put his arms around her. "Now come here and let me kiss you."

And he did.

Christina and Dana spent Christmas Day at the Millard household. It was a wonderful day, full of warm, fuzzy feelings and lots of laughter. Dana made fast friends with Nicole, who kept asking her for advice on her clothes and her hair and, of course, about boys, most of whom were complete jerks in Nicole's opinion and so-o-o imma*chure*.

Nicole was a lovely girl, open and direct, and Christina was relieved that both she and Matthew had so readily accepted her presence in their father's life. Horror stories abounded about the evil that kids would create in these situations, but there was no sign of it from these two.

It was a happy time, and Christina told herself to live in the present. She would enjoy every minute of Jack's attentions and refuse to harbor any thoughts about what might happen in the future and about the heartache that might follow.

But she didn't quite manage it, of course. Lurking in the back of her mind, there was always the fear—like an evil little devil hiding in dark corners, then jumping out to terrorize her at unexpected moments.

"I think it would be real cool if you and Dad got married," Nicole said one evening, and out jumped the evil little devil. Nicole was going to a party and Christina was braiding her dark hair into a sleek French braid. Christina's hands stilled for a moment and her heart began to race.

"You do?" she said noncommittally, hoping her voice sounded natural.

"Yeah. Then Dana would be my stepsister and you my stepmom. I think I'd really like that, though my friend, Amy, says I'm crazy. Her father got married again last year and she doesn't like her stepmother at all because she's always nagging her about her room and her clothes and stuff and they're always fighting."

"That doesn't sound very good," Christina said, her hands automatically continuing with her task.

"I don't think we'd fight a lot, do you? Would you tell me to clean up my room?"

Christina smiled at that. "No. I think you're old enough to take responsibility for your own room. That's what I used to tell Dana. Boy, her room was a disaster sometimes, but I'd just close the door so I wouldn't have to see it and eventually she always cleaned it up and now she's really quite neat."

"That's cool." Nicole grinned into the mirror and Christina smiled back at her reflection.

"You've got beautiful hair," she said. "And it looks very nice like this, away from your face."

"Thank you. I'm glad you're here to help me." Nicole shifted a little on the dressing-table stool. "I think you and Dad should get married," she stated again. "I know he'd like it. He's crazy about you and he seems so happy. Do you want to marry him?''

Her heart lurched painfully. ''Marriage is a serious commitment, Nicole,'' she said carefully.

''You promise to love each other and you really mean it. And when things get really tough, you always stick it out together because you are each other's best friend and you never give up on each other.'' Nicole grinned. ''That's what Dad says it is and I think he knows. He really loved my mom, you know.''

Christina felt a constriction in her throat. ''Yes, I know,'' she said, glancing at the photo hanging by Nicole's bed. It was an interesting profile shot of Sara, her smiling face tilted upward to look at something above her, showing a perfect little nose and a long, slender neck. Rich, dark hair cascaded over her shoulders and down her back. Sara was beautiful.

She glanced back in the mirror, meeting Nicole's solemn gaze.

''I think he really loves you now,'' Nicole said. ''I asked him, and he said yes.''

Christina felt as if she had no air to breathe. She didn't want to have this conversation with Nicole. Desperately she searched her mind to find a way to distract her, but Nicole wasn't a little girl she could sidetrack with a dish of ice cream. The expression on her face was open and honest and determined. She wouldn't allow herself to be distracted like a toddler. Christina bit her lip. Well, she could try, couldn't she?

''I'm just about done,'' she said, twisting the last of the hair into the braid. ''Do you have a rubber band or a clip?''

''Do you love my dad?'' Nicole asked as if she hadn't even heard what she'd said. Christina fought the urge to simply flee the room.

''Of course I do,'' she said lightly.

"I mean, do you *really, truly* love him?"

Her mouth went dry; her heart stumbled. It was ridiculous that the questions of this girl, this child, could disturb her nervous system so. She didn't have to answer the question, of course. She could lie, be evasive, but it went against every fiber of her being to lie to this girl who had accepted her into her life and offered her trust. She swallowed, feeling as if she had a noose around her neck.

"Yes, I do," she said.

Nicole's serious face broke out in a triumphant smile. "I knew it! Well, then, why don't you get married?"

"It's not so simple, Nicole. It's something that—"

"Why not? If you really love each other, why is it hard to promise you'll be there for each other always?"

"There are other things involved sometimes, Nicole. I'm finished and I do need a rubber band. Do you have one handy?" Her hands were trembling.

Nicole opened a drawer and rummaged in it while Christina held on to the end of the finished braid. Over Nicole's bent head, she stared blindly into the mirror, until movement caught her eye. Jack appeared in the open doorway.

"You know what I think?" Nicole asked as she fished out a pink rubber band and handed it to Christina. "I think you're scared or something. Dana told me that her father cheated on you. Dad would never do that, you know. Never!"

"Hello there, ladies," Jack said, coming into the room. Christina wasn't sure if she was relieved or mortified. She didn't know what he might have heard.

"Dad! Isn't it true that you would never cheat on Christina if you were married?"

Christina groaned inwardly. Oh, great, she thought, this is really great. Getting better all the time.

Jack offered a crooked little smile. "I wouldn't cheat on her, married or not." He rubbed his knuckles against his daughter's cheek. "And you, sweetheart, look very lovely."

"Thank you." Nicole glanced up at her father and gave him a challenging look. "And I think it would be really cool if you got married."

"I appreciate your enthusiasm," he said dryly, "but now you'd better scoot. Your ride is here."

Nicole leaped to her feet. "They're early!" she wailed indignantly as she raced out the door. "Bye! See you later!"

Christina wiped her clammy hands on the pink towel Nicole had used to dry her hair. It was sopping wet and didn't do her hands any good. Neither did Jack's dark gaze.

He took the towel from her hands. "So," he said lightly, "you think I'd cheat on you?"

Her stomach churned and she clenched her hands into fists. "Dana apparently told Nicole that my ex-husband cheated on me. Your daughter was making sure I knew you wouldn't do that, ever."

His mouth curved up at the corners. "Filial love, it's a wonderful thing." He put one arm around her. "It's rather touching, isn't it, for her to want us to be married?"

Christina froze. She couldn't help it. She also couldn't prevent him from feeling her reaction.

He frowned at her. "For heaven's sake, Christina," he said on a low note, "'married' isn't a dirty word."

She couldn't meet his gaze. "I'm sorry," she muttered.

He looked at her for a long moment, then propelled her out of the room. "Dinner's ready," he said evenly.

New Year's Eve arrived. They wished each other a very happy New Year and kissed each other lovingly, but as they did so, Christina was aware of the evil little devil leaping around the edges of her consciousness, snickering.

It was the middle of January and the snow lay thick and soft on the fields and woods. It looked like a picture postcard. Even in winter, her place was beautiful. Christina was happy.

When Jack left on an extended business trip to the Far East, she was determined not to be miserable. She had spent years without the company of a man; she could certainly do it again. She could read books and magazines. Rent videos. Clean out her closets. Certainly she was not addicted to him, was she?

Well, maybe only a little bit, she had to admit after he'd been gone several days. She missed his lovemaking and the devilish gleam in his eyes. She missed his cheerful manner, his sense of humor.

Staring at the snowy landscape one afternoon, she catalogued all his good qualities, every one of which she was missing sorely. He was a perfect man, a perfect lover. And he seemed to think she was perfect, too. Imagine that! She was so lucky.

The phone disturbed her mental rhapsody. She answered it with a sigh, feeling bliss make a fast escape at the sound of Anne Marie's doom-filled voice. Christina dragged in a fortifying breath. There had been many calls and many distressing stories about her nephew, Jason, who seemed to have lost his mind.

"We've made a decision," Anne Marie said, her voice quivering. "We can't wait until he ends up in juvenile detention or takes all of us with him into the madhouse. We're going to put him in a private residential school, just for kids like him. We found one that I think will do him good."

"Oh, Anne Marie," Christina whispered, shocked.

"Nothing else is working!" her sister wailed. "We don't know what to do with him! The school doesn't know what to do with him! The therapist doesn't know what to do with him! We have to do *something*!"

"Of course, of course! Can you afford it?"

"No, not from our regular income." There was a silence. Christina heard Anne Marie take in a deep breath. "Christina, I don't know how to ask you this, but..."

"But what?" Glancing out the window, she noticed storm clouds gathering. She felt the clouds gathering inside herself, too—a sure sign of impending doom.

"Is there any way you can buy out my share in Sleepy Hollow?"

Christina's heart sank like a rock in a pond. "Buy you out?" she repeated as if she didn't understand.

"Yes."

"I...I don't know. I took out a second mortgage to add another bedroom and update the bathrooms two years ago. I...I just don't know, Anne Marie. I have to sit down and look at the numbers."

"Would you, please? It's the only asset I have that's worth anything. We'll pay the first year's tuition out of our retirement fund, but we can't figure out where to get the rest, and he'll have to be in that school for a while, I'm sure."

Numb with shock, Christina put the phone down a few minutes later. She wouldn't need to do a lot of figuring and number crunching to know that she couldn't possibly afford to buy Anne Marie out. As a matter of fact, she didn't need to do any at all. The place was too heavily mortgaged for the banks to give her another loan and she had no money of her own stashed away somewhere.

The day passed in a blur. Her mind was racing in her frantic efforts to think of a solution. She wanted to help.

There was no doubt in her mind that if Anne Marie said Jason needed a special residential school, he needed one. And if her sister needed help, then she would do anything in her power to give it to her.

It took her several days of agonizing, but eventually she had to admit to herself that there was only one solution, no matter how hard it was.

She had to sell the inn.

Dana was home for the weekend, and over a cup of tea, Christina told her about Jason and about what needed to be done.

Dana was aghast. "But, Mom, what are you going to do?"

"I'll have to find a job," she said bravely. She didn't even want to think about it. It made her stomach churn with anxiety. How was she, a middle-aged woman, going to find a job? Everybody knew it was hard and she didn't even have a college degree.

Stop it! Stop it! she told herself. Something would turn up as long as she could keep a positive attitude.

Dana looked uncomfortable. "Have you... have you thought of asking Jack to help you? Maybe he'll give you a loan."

Christina stiffened. "No," she said flatly. "Absolutely, positively no."

"Don't you think he'd want to help you?"

"That's not the point. I don't want to be in his debt." I'd rather scrub floors, she added silently.

"Maybe he could buy Aunt Anne Marie's share. Then you wouldn't be in his debt."

"He'd be my partner." What a nightmare of an idea! He could come in at any moment and tell her he didn't like pink tablecloths. He wanted green. He could argue about her choice of wines, about the price of the rooms. Not that she actually thought he might do that, but the possibility was always there. She'd leave herself open to his interference. "I wouldn't be independent anymore," she added.

Dana's face softened. "Would that be so terrible, Mom?"

Christina stared at her pretty daughter, feeling her body tense with instinctive fear. A wave of memories flooded back. Peter telling her he didn't like the yellow dress, didn't like the way she cooked the chicken, didn't like the books she read, didn't like the way she raised Dana. A wave of memories, a rising tide of panic. She nodded. "Yes, it would be terrible. I couldn't bear it."

Jack called her from Hong Kong that same evening, telling her he was in the Regency, sitting in a room overlooking the harbor, and wished she were with him.

"Tell me what it looks like," she asked. "I'll close my eyes and pretend I'm there with you."

So he told her all about the luxurious room, the big bed, the marble bathroom. "There's a huge whirlpool bath," he elaborated, "also with a view of the harbor, and I'm having very disturbing visions of you and me in it together, covered in bubbles, sipping champagne and feeding each other strawberries."

She laughed. "How decadent."

"Mmm. Get on a plane and see how decadent it can get."

"I wish I could." And the thought occurred to her that in a few months she would no longer be running the inn, that in a few months she might have more freedom, might actually be able to do something crazy like getting on a plane to Hong Kong on a whim and sitting in a whirlpool bath with Jack.

For one crazy moment, she wanted to tell Jack about her having to sell the inn—a moment of temptation, of fear and longing. A moment of weakness.

"Tell me about you," he said. "How have you been?"

"Lonely," she said, which was the truth. "I miss you." Which was also the truth.

"Me, too," he said. "I'm thinking about you all the time."

They talked for a while and she managed to hold on to her courage and didn't tell him about selling the inn. Having finished the conversation, Christina went back to perusing the paper looking for jobs.

He called her every day, and every day it was more difficult not to tell him what was going on. She lied to him, saying everything was fine. She lied to him when he asked if anything new had happened. She lied to him when he asked if anything was wrong. Every time he called, her heart leaped to her throat. She missed him. She longed for him to be back, to throw herself in his arms, to beg him to save her.

"I've been thinking," Dana said a week later. "This situation isn't really a problem, Mom. Not if you don't want to look at it that way."

Christina gave her daughter a suspicious look. "If it isn't a problem, then what is it?"

"An opportunity. There are no problems," Dana intoned sagely. "Only opportunities."

Christina rolled her eyes. "Thank you for your wisdom. I can just imagine my opportunities. Abject poverty, welfare, food stamps, roach-infested apartments."

"It helps to have a bit of self-esteem and a positive attitude," Dana said blandly.

Christina groaned, then laughed. "All right, all right. I suppose I could land myself a job as a chef in a luxury resort hotel in the Bahamas, living quarters included in the pay. Sunshine every day. What a life."

"Hawaii wouldn't be bad, either, or the Fiji Islands."

"Or Tahiti, or Bali."

"Just imagine," Dana said longingly. "I'd come and visit." She sighed. "But you'd better make it the Bahamas or Bermuda or I won't be able to pay the airfare. And Jack could fly over in his private jet whenever he felt like it. Or had you forgotten about him?"

No, she had not forgotten about him. Part of her— the weak, scared part of her—wanted desperately to ask him for help. He would want to, she was sure. He would want to give her a loan, take charge, do anything that needed to be done. Another part—the strong, independent part—was determined she would deal with this crisis without him.

And she would. She *was* strong. She *was* independent. She could take care of herself.

Two weeks later, it was all arranged, quickly and efficiently, as if it had been meant to be this way. As if the whole process had been ready and waiting for Christina to set it in motion. The new owners would be Carl and his wife, Gina, who were out of their minds with happiness to be able to buy the inn. A dream come true! A miracle!

It was nice to see them so delighted. No matter how awful it was to give up the inn, Christina was relieved she didn't have to hand it over to a stranger.

She was determined not to drown herself in a sea of depression and negativity. She'd gone that route when her marriage broke up and it was not an experience worth repeating. She was going to confront this new phase in her life with positive thinking and the knowledge that she was a confident, competent person. She was so brave, so courageous, and she was proud of herself. After all, hadn't there been many times when she had longed for more freedom?

Now she had freedom.

So much freedom, in fact, that it scared her to death. She had visions of herself on welfare, buying clothes in secondhand stores, living in a rat-ridden apartment in a dangerous part of the city.

She stared at her blurred image in the mirror. So why was she crying? She hadn't cried once up to now. There was no reason to cry.

She stared outside at the peaceful, snowy landscape. In the moonlight, it looked calm and serene. On impulse, she pulled on her boots, coat and gloves and stepped out into the frigid night. She needed to calm her mind, to find some peace. Her boots crunched in the dry snow as she walked toward the woods. Breathing in the clean, cold air, she walked along the paths by the pond, through the woods, trying to soak up the quiet of the moonlit evening. Finally, cold and tired, she sat down on an old wooden bench, which had been cleared of snow by the gardener, and hugged herself.

She felt lonely, so utterly lonely, and the tears came again. She let them fall. It didn't matter. There was no one to see or hear her here and it was better to let them out than bottle them up.

She didn't know how long she sat there, hunched in her coat, feeling sorry for herself and her trials, when she heard a voice. Someone calling her name. And then she saw the beam of a flashlight dancing along the path.

"Christina!"

Her heart began to gallop. "I'm here," she said, but her voice didn't carry. It was merely a throaty whisper. Jack. Jack had come back. And then he was there, on his haunches in front of her.

"Christina! What on earth are you doing out here at this hour! You're frozen!"

"You're back," she murmured. For a moment, she wondered if she was only imagining him there, if her longing for comfort and succor had conjured him up in her mind, but she knew it was real when he pulled her into his arms and she felt the warmth of his face against her icy cheek.

"It's past ten! What are you doing out here by yourself?"

She swallowed. "I took a walk. It's so beautiful here." Her voice sounded thick and she knew he'd hear it.

"Have you been crying?" He sounded shocked. "What's wrong, Christina?"

"I'm fine," she lied, and shivered. "I didn't expect you. You came home early."

"I wanted to surprise you." He kissed her cold lips, his mouth warm and reassuring. "Oh, God," he muttered, "let's get you inside before you freeze to death."

They walked back to the cabin in silence and she sat in front of the wood stove, trying to warm up while Jack was in the kitchen making them both hot chocolate. She would have to tell him and she wasn't looking forward to it.

"Something's obviously wrong," he said as he handed her the mug. "Out with it."

She took a deep breath. She wasn't going to break down again. She would tell him the truth matter-of-factly.

"I'm selling the inn to Carl and Gina."

He looked stunned. "You're selling the inn? Why?"

She took a sip of the hot chocolate and told him why in a few carefully chosen businesslike sentences, her voice as calm as she could manage. He didn't say anything, just sat there looking at her.

"It's working out very well," she said. "Carl and Gina are selling their house and getting their financial situation in order and they'll take over in March. That will give me time to find a job and a place to live." She was beginning to feel warm. "It's not what I had planned, of course, but it's an opportunity to do something different, to have some more freedom. Maybe I'll get a chance to travel." She smiled bravely. "And have many exciting adventures," she added with a touch of drama.

"And you're so delighted, you walk out into the snow and sit crying on a bench until you're practically frozen to death," he said evenly. "Perfect."

"I was merely being sentimental. My parents started this place and I helped them, and it's been all mine for four years and I was happy here. What's so terrible about being a little sentimental about that?" It sounded very reasonable to her own ears.

He gave her a long look as if he were seeing into her soul. He didn't answer her question, just stood there staring at her and his silence made her nervous.

"You didn't tell me any of this was going on," he said finally, his voice oddly toneless. "I called you every day while I was gone and you never said anything."

"It was my problem and I knew what I had to do," she said, feeling a sudden trepidation at the dark shadows in his eyes.

There was silence once more, a terrible silence that made her nerves jump. She saw the tense line of his jaw, the anger in his eyes. A tremor ran through her.

His gaze locked with hers. "This doesn't make any sense," he said in a low, controlled voice. "Why didn't you tell me?"

CHAPTER TEN

CHRISTINA'S stomach clenched painfully and she fought for calmness. "There was no need." Her voice sounded nervous in her own ears.

"I could have helped you."

That's what she had been afraid of. She swallowed. "I knew what I had to do," she said again.

"*Sell* the place?" His voice was hard and angry. "Good God, Christina! There are other solutions!"

"I know," she said. "But I chose this one."

He stared at her. "Did you sign anything? Can you get out of it?"

She gritted her teeth. "I don't want to get out of it, Jack."

He shoved his hands into his pockets. "Dammit, Christina!" he said roughly. "Why? You love this place! There's no *need* for you to sell it! There are all sorts of other ways to deal with this problem!"

She anchored her feet to the floor, feeling her heart begin to race. "I dealt with it in the way *I* saw fit!"

"Why didn't you talk to me first? Why didn't you ask me for help?"

"Because I didn't *want* to."

Her words reverberated in the silent room. He looked at her, his eyes bleak. "I see," he said then, his voice low and bitter. "You don't trust me. You still don't trust me."

"Jack, I didn't—"

He turned away and strode to the door. "I'd better go." His voice was flat and dead.

"Jack, please!"

He didn't stop. He opened the door and was gone.

Christina stood rooted to the floor. She wanted to run after him, tell him not to be angry, to stay with her, tell him she needed him.

No, she didn't need him. She didn't want to need him. This situation was her problem and she would handle it. She could take care of herself. And if he could not understand it, then that was his problem.

Such brave thoughts.

Only she didn't feel brave at all. Not with that lump in her throat, not with the terror squeezing her heart.

Unable to move, she heard the car rev up and crunch down the driveway. Her throat ached and tears ran down her face. Tears of new grief and old sorrows and the knowledge that nothing was easy.

She had hurt him, and that had never been her intention. You don't trust me, he had said. You still don't trust me.

The bitterness of the words hung in the air, wrenching at her heart.

Hands clamped on the steering wheel, Jack maneuvered the car down the snowy road, his body tense with anger and rejection. What was the matter with this woman? Why hadn't she wanted to talk to him about her problem? What the hell had possessed her to offer the inn to Carl without consulting anybody?

His stomach churned. She was giving up the inn, the place she loved. He slammed his hand hard on the steering wheel. He couldn't allow it. He would do anything for her. He could buy the inn himself, or just her sister's share. To make things even easier, he could simply pay the damn school tuition for the kid, for all he cared.

Whatever she had signed, he could get her out of it.

I don't want to get out of it, she'd said. And she hadn't wanted his help. He cursed in frustration.

He shifted in his seat and stared into the night. His head ached. God, this is not what he had expected—to be driving home at this godforsaken hour of the night. He'd wanted to be with her, hold her in his arms, make love to her. The past three weeks had seemed interminable. He had ached for her with an intensity he did not know he was capable of. He needed her. He wanted her in his life.

But she didn't want him—not enough, not really. She didn't want to be his wife. She didn't want his help. There was always that distance, that odd fear in her eyes. And when the subject of marriage came up, she practically freaked out.

Not exactly an ego booster, this, he thought wryly. You'd better figure out how to deal with it, man.

The house was as quiet as a tomb when he came through the door. The kids were already asleep. He poured himself a stiff drink and sat in his study and tried to think.

In the far reaches of his memory, he suddenly heard her voice, the words she had said months ago: *I need my independence. I'm never giving it up.*

That's why she hadn't told him. That's why she'd wanted to deal with her problems by herself. Because once, she'd been married to a man who'd squeezed the life out of her, who'd told her what to do, what to wear, what to say, what to think. And no one was ever going to come close enough to do it again. No one. And that included him.

He gulped down the last of the whiskey and tried not to feel the searing rejection. Right now he'd better just accept the situation for what it was. The worst thing he could do was to try to change Christina's mind and force her to accept his help. He'd have to let her handle her affairs in her own way. She'd find a job and start over. She was bright and talented and something would come up. If only it could be something that she'd enjoy, that would give her the opportunity to use her talents.

He went to bed and slept restlessly, his dreams confused and tortured, until out of the turmoil flashed an idea that woke him up with its brilliance. He stared into the darkness and smiled.

Christina loved her bed and she loved sleeping, but the night was sheer misery. When the phone rang early the next morning and she heard Jack on the other end of the line, relief made her almost giddy.

"Oh, Jack," she said, her voice quavering, "I didn't mean to hurt your feelings. I just—"

"It's all right, Christina. I want you to know that I don't mean to interfere with your life. I simply wanted to help, but if selling the inn is what you decide to do, then I'll respect your decision."

She swallowed. His words sounded so good. "Thank you," she said, tears blurring her vision. "I'm sorry I upset you last night."

"I'll live. Don't worry about it."

"I had a rotten night."

He laughed. "That makes two of us. We should have been together in the same bed. It would have prevented the problem."

She closed her eyes. "Yes."

"Do you have any plans for today?"

It was Wednesday and she was off. "I'm cleaning out closets today."

"Would you like some help?"

She smiled into the phone. "Yes, I would."

He drove up to her cabin a little after three, wearing boots, jeans and a leather jacket over a heavy sweater. Her heart leaped to her throat as she saw him stride to the front door. No matter what he wore—expensive city clothes or casual gear—he looked so handsome, so vibrant and strong.

She opened the door and he wrapped himself around her wordlessly, nudging the door shut behind them with his foot. He kissed her, a deep, hungry kiss that sent her senses reeling.

"I'm sorry I got mad last night," he whispered. "My male pride, I suppose. My poor ego, all busted up because you didn't want my help."

"I didn't mean to hurt your feelings."

"I know, but I'm over it now." He kissed her again, giving a low moan in his throat. "I missed you. I want you."

In the bedroom, they took off each other's clothes, fumbling, groping, laughing—silly with desire. They fell into bed, kissing each other drunkenly.

"I love you," he said between kisses, his voice husky with arousal.

"I love you, too." It felt so good to say the words, to mean them and treasure them.

His hands and mouth were eager on her body, feverish with waiting—stroking, tasting. She loved him back with all her own impatient need and they moved together in a primitive, erotic dance.

She loved his body, the smooth skin over hard muscles, the taste and scent of him. Her blood sang, and the dance went on and on, faster and faster. Until the fire was doused and they lay still in each other's arms, spent.

Christina felt the thudding of his heart against her cheek. His chest was strong and solid, like all of him. She kissed his damp skin and smiled. Her body felt rich and heavy with languor and she sighed and closed her eyes.

Slowly, strength came creeping back into her sated, exhausted body. She gazed drowsily at the clock. It was just after four. "Teatime," she said.

He kissed the top of her head and laughed. "Holy time. May nothing ever interfere with your afternoon tea."

She sat up and ran her hands through her hair. "It's in my genes. I can't help it."

"Your genes? Oh, yes, your proper English granny."

"Tea is very restorative. And after you so expertly ravished me, I need to be revived." She slipped out of bed.

He laughed. "If tea will do it, I'm all for it."

So she wrapped a kimono around her and made a pot of Earl Grey tea and set out pretty cups and a plate of Carl's delicious lemon tarts. And they sat in the sitting room in front of a roaring fire in the wood stove, surrounded by the chaos she had created earlier that day by cleaning out closets and turning over drawers.

And very unfortunately, right there on top of a jumble of papers was a picture of Peter and ten-year-old Dana in front of their house. A beautiful house, a beautiful child, a beautiful husband.

A faithless husband. A miserable excuse for a man.

"Nice house," Jack said, glancing at the photo.

She sighed melodramatically. "The gilded cage," she said, then shook her head. "No, it was no cage. I only thought it was. I was a prisoner of my own misconceptions. Poor me. So, one day, I opened the door and realized it had never been locked, and I flew away. Free as a bird."

"So easy, so simple," he said evenly.

She sighed. "No, not easy, not simple. But possible anyway, and I finally did it and I've never regretted it."

"Why did you marry him?" he asked.

"Because I was in love with him. Because I was naive and stupid."

Because he made me feel good, she added silently.

In the beginning he had. He had made her feel . . . special. He had told her she was beautiful and he had taken her out to buy clothes and given her jewelry. He had bragged about her to his friends, saying she spoke three languages and had traveled the world, as if this made her a better person. His friends' girlfriends didn't speak three languages and had never been out of their own state. It had been a little amusing at first, and it had made her feel good that he was proud of her, or at least that's what it had seemed to her.

At the time, it hadn't occurred to her that he had never mentioned the fact to his friends that she was a volunteer at the Sunset Retirement Home, where she spent time with lonely people—reading to them, playing games, talking. Not that that necessarily made her a better person, either, but it said something more meaningful about her than the fact that she spoke three languages. Not until much later had she been able to figure out what really had been going on. He had wanted her beautiful and sophisticated to boost his own ego, to show her off to his friends and family, to make everybody think he was a great guy to have such a great woman.

Once they'd been married, she'd kept on trying to please him, wearing the kind of clothes he wanted her to wear, cooking the food he wanted to eat. The house was a showplace and she kept it immaculate. But slowly, little by little, he started complaining about her.

Nothing she did was ever good enough. She hadn't understood that her husband was a man secretly insecure about himself and that by putting her down, he thought he was making himself look better. It didn't work, of course, and so in the end he tried to prove himself by going out with other women. He slowly, insidiously, undermined her self-confidence, and because he fooled around with other women, it was her womanly side that suffered most.

"In what way were you naive?" Jack asked.

She shrugged. "I didn't realize that he just saw mc as a piece of property that he owned, something that was good for his image." She grimaced. "Or not so good. Anyway, I don't want to talk about him. He's in the past. Hand me another lemon tart, will you?"

He handed her another lemon tart. "So," he said casually, "in March you're going to be a woman of leisure. No more inn, no more managing and cooking. What are you planning to do?"

"I'm going to find a job." She took a bite of the tart.

"I have one for you."

She gave him a suspicious look. "I don't want it," she said with her mouth full.

"You don't even know what it is."

"I don't want handouts."

He gave a long-suffering sigh. "I knew that's what you were going to say."

She took a leisurely sip of tea. "Then why did you even bother to ask?"

"Because it's absolutely perfect. The perfect job for you. You would love it. And I need you to take it because there's no one who'd do it better."

She put the cup and saucer back on the coffee table. "Don't tell me you've fired Mrs. Dawkins and you want me to move in with you and play housekeeper, cook and mistress all rolled into one."

He quirked a brow, his expression one of consideration. "Mmm. That's even better. I hadn't thought of that."

"Well, you can forget that one, too." She leaned forward and picked up the teapot. "I don't intend to be anybody's kept woman, married or otherwise, ever again. More tea?''

"I would love some, thank you." He held out his cup and smiled charmingly. "You still don't want to marry me?''

"No," she said, pouring tea. "You'd marry me and I'd feel indebted to you for the rest of my life because you rescued me from poverty and deprivation." She put the teapot down on the table and leaned back against the sofa cushions. "I can see the tabloids already: Wealthy Industrialist Marries Middle-aged Divorcée Down On Her Luck. Or something worse. You know how awful those rags are. They'd say all kinds of horrible things. They'd put us on the front cover and they wouldn't bother to retouch my wrinkles and I'd look like an old hag and—''

"Shut up, Christina." He kissed her on the mouth to silence her. "Sooner or later I am going to marry you, you know," he said against her lips. "So you might as well stop all this self-flagellation. You are *not* old. You do *not* have wrinkles, you—''

"I do, too," she said

"Well, I don't see any."

"That's because you aren't looking."

"That's because I don't care. Besides, I have wrinkles and gray hair and—''

"It looks very sexy, very distinguished."

He groaned. "You're driving me crazy. I need a drink."

"I just poured you more tea."

"That'll do it," he said dryly.

They finished the whole pot of tea, talking about Matthew, who had won a science project, about Nicole, who had a boyfriend with an earring in one ear and a tattoo on his arm, and about his French grandmother, who was turning ninety years old in May and had summoned the family to France to help her celebrate. And all the while, in the back of her mind, Christina wondered about the job he'd offered her, what it could possibly be. They went for a walk and had dinner and after that Christina couldn't hold out any longer. Her curiosity was killing her, and with two glasses of wine, her obstinacy had evaporated.

"So tell me about that job," she said lightly.

He filled her glass. "You said you didn't want it."

"I don't even know what it is." She took a sip of the wine. "But if you really need me, I might consider it." She smiled sweetly. "As a favor," she added generously.

"Of course," he said, trying not to smile.

"If the pay is good, that is."

"It's very, very good."

"And if I can be my own boss. I don't want anybody telling me what to do."

"You can be your own boss."

"Sounds perfect," she said, taking another drink of wine. She was feeling pleasantly relaxed and generous of spirit.

"It is," he agreed.

"So what's the catch? If something sounds too good to be true, it usually is."

He looked solemn. "There's no catch. It's a job, with good pay, time off, and you'll be your own boss. You can make your own schedule, everything."

"Too good to be true."

He leaned back and studied her. "Would you like to know what it is?"

She waved her hand in a casual gesture. "Sure."

"Do you remember the country estate I mentioned a few months ago?" he asked.

She nodded. "Yes. I saw the pictures. You told me they're busy restoring and remodeling it."

"Right. It's expected to be finished next month. Then you come in to furnish and decorate it, and when that's done, you stay to run the place, hire a staff and take charge of the kitchen and the menu."

She grew very still. Perfect, he had said. And it was.

He stroked her hair, then gently pulled her face closer to his and looked into her eyes. "You'd do such a wonderful job, Christina. You have so much talent and creativity. I wouldn't want anybody else for this job."

Her heart stumbled, her blood warmed.

He kissed her softly. "Please, say yes."

She said yes.

CHAPTER ELEVEN

AZALEAS bloomed in a glorious celebration of spring. The Garden of Eden, Christina thought as she slowly walked through the newly landscaped gardens surrounding the Millard country estate she had so carefully furnished and decorated in the past two months. Because of the Millard name, the refurbishing of the colonial country estate was receiving quite a bit of attention, and because she was doing the interior, so was she. Local papers and a couple of magazines had already done write-ups about the estate, and a Philadelphia TV station wanted to do a piece, as well. The interest had surprised and amazed her.

But the phone call she had received that morning had been even more amazing and she couldn't wait to tell Jack, who should be here any moment now to pick her up. Joy bubbled inside her frothy as champagne. Her step light, she sashayed along the path, back to her own little stone house, a cottage really, that sat secluded within a stand of tall pines not far from the main house. She felt like dancing, singing. It was so incredible!

What a day! And as if things weren't good enough already, they were even getting better. In a few hours, she and Jack and his kids would be winging their way across the Atlantic Ocean to France.

Jack's cobalt blue car came sailing up the main driveway, slowing down as he turned into the narrow lane leading to her little house. He pulled to a smooth stop right beside her, opened the door and leaped out with a grin. He looked lean and fit in his jeans and black short-sleeved shirt, and her heart skipped happily at the sight of him. She would never get enough of looking at him.

He hugged and kissed her. "You seem ready to burst into song," he said warmly. "What's up?"

"I have something to tell you," she said, feeling her excitement almost flow over. "It's absolutely fantastic. You won't believe it!"

"What is it?"

"In the car. I'll tell you in the car."

"All right. Are you ready?" His gaze caught her suitcase waiting by the front door and his grin widened. "Really, really ready, I see. Well, you deserve a vacation." He kissed her again. "You'll have to do absolutely nothing except laze on the beach, eat olives and pâté de foie gras and peasant bread to your heart's content. And of course, take drives into the countryside with me and smile at my *grand-mère* once in a while."

His French grandmother was turning ninety years old and the family was gathering at her large villa in the south of France to celebrate the event. And she, Christina, was invited to join the festivities. Meeting all of Jack's various relatives en masse was a daunting prospect, but Jack had assured her they were all wonderful people who would invite her into the fold with open arms and love in their hearts.

Christina didn't think she was a cynic, but this she had to see.

"You mean your entire family—aunts, uncles, brothers, in-laws, are wonderful people, every single one of them?"

"Absolutely." He looked a bit smug. "Which is not to say we don't have our share of oddballs."

"You being one of them?" she asked nicely.

He laughed. "Me? You haven't seen anything yet. Wait till you meet my granny."

"Don't scare me off," she muttered.

But going to the south of France was an adventure, and she had to admit she was looking forward to it in spite of the suspiciously angelic relatives. She'd been sprucing up her once-fluent French and hoped it wouldn't disgrace her too much.

Jack put her suitcase in the car and moments later they zoomed down the road toward the airport. Christina sat back and relaxed and gave a contented sigh.

Jack put his hand briefly on her knee. "So tell me the fantastic news," he urged. "My curiosity is killing me."

"Oh, yes," she said casually. "I had a job offer this morning."

His brows quirked up as he gave her a quick sideways glance. "Really? What was it?"

"To furnish and decorate a two-hundred-year-old plantation house in South Carolina," she said, trying to sound cool and businesslike. "They've restored it and made it into a country hotel. It has slave quarters that have been refurbished as guest rooms. They offered to fly me out to take a look at it before I have to make up my mind." Her effort at nonchalance failed completely. Her voice began to ring with enthusiasm. "They liked what I've done at the estate and now they want me to work for them! Isn't it fantastic?"

The offer had bowled her over completely. After the initial surprise, pride and joy had flooded her. This was so great! Her work was being recognized! Valued! It had been in the papers and now other people wanted her to work for them, as well. She'd felt jubilant.

She still felt jubilant. She was aware she was grinning at Jack like a fool, but she couldn't help herself.

He laughed. "I so like to see you enthusiastic," he said. "But I'm not at all surprised, you know."

"You're not?"

"Do you think I'm the only one in the world who recognizes your talents?"

"I guess not." She grinned. "Anyway, I am not taking the job, of course."

"Why not?" he asked evenly.

"Because I like the one I have even better—managing the estate and cooking for retreats and gatherings." In another month, the place would be ready to accommodate guests, and she was looking forward to the new work now that most of the furnishing and decorating had been completed.

"Are you sure?"

"Of course I'm sure! I'm just excited I have real choices!" She studied his calm profile. "Would you object to my going to South Carolina for a few months?"

He arched his brow. "Object? No, I wouldn't dream of it. I wouldn't *like* it. As a matter of fact, I'd hate like hell to have you be so far away." He sighed heavily. "I'd probably wither away with loneliness and spend my nights gambling or drinking, but I'd respect your freedom to make your own decisions. You shouldn't have to worry about me."

"Thank you," she said solemnly. "I'll remember that."

He kept his gaze securely focused on the traffic, which was getting heavier and heavier, but he reached out and touched her hand briefly. "What I want is for you to do what makes you happy," he said, his tone serious.

"Working at the estate will make me happy," she returned, feeling an upwelling of emotion. "And being with you."

She loved him and life was wonderful. She wanted it to stay this way forever. She wanted nothing to change.

If only the little devil hiding in her mind would stop haunting her, whispering that things would surely change.

* * *

Much to her surprise, Jack's supposedly marvelous relatives were really quite wonderful, accepting her without reservation and making her comfortable in the family and in the sprawling, tile-roofed villa that hugged the cliffs overlooking the azure Mediterranean Sea. It was a magnificent house with arched doorways, cool tile floors and spacious, airy rooms. Books, plants and artwork enlivened the living spaces. Christina admired the wonderful antique furniture, the exquisite Oriental rugs, the fresh, fragrant flowers from the garden that perfumed every room. Most importantly, it was a house filled with the sounds of happy people talking and laughing. Jack's grandmother, whom everyone called Nana, was a vivacious old lady with the devil in her eyes. She loved young blood, she told Christina, and found old people with all their aches and pains so boring. Apparently, she herself did not suffer from aches and pains.

Among the magnificent works of art, Christina found a large, framed photograph of Nana and two of her great-grandchildren, babies then, squirming on her lap, struggling to get off and be free. A poignant contrast of old age and youth. It was a photo to make you smile.

"It's beautiful," Christina said to Jack. It was the truth, of course. It was a magnificent picture.

"Yes, it is," he agreed.

"She was so talented," Jack's sister-in-law, Lisa, said with a sigh. She was standing next to them in front of the photo, a glass of wine in her hand. She was a tall redhead with pale skin and freckles and a lovely, engaging smile. "And such a generous, beautiful person, too," she added, gazing at the picture. "At times like this, I still miss seeing her with her camera, having a ball."

Christina's mouth went dry. She'd been here only two days and Sara's name kept coming up—people telling Nicole how much she looked like her mother, talking about memories of years gone by—what Sara had said or done. And now the photo and more about Sara.

Why was it so hard to hear good things about this woman? It made her feel mean and jealous and she didn't like to feel that way, didn't *want* to feel that way.

Lisa looked warmly at Christina. "But we're all so glad Jack's found you." She glanced over at Jack, smiling. "You seem awfully happy—Christina must be good for you."

He put an arm around Christina and grinned at Lisa. "She's very, very good for me."

"I made a mistake," Jack said. "I shouldn't have married you." He sounded like a stranger, as if his voice was not really his. "You're not good for me, not anymore. I need somebody different."

Somebody different, somebody different. The evil little devil, dressed in red, danced around her, laughing.

Different how? she wanted to ask, but her tongue wouldn't move, paralyzed by an anguish that permeated her entire body.

She kept trying to speak, to say she loved him, but all she could do was cry and cry.

Her face was wet with tears when she awoke, her body curled up in misery. Darkness surrounded her, and for a moment she thought she might have died of grief. Then she became aware of being in bed, of Jack's sleeping body next to her, and the distress ebbed out of her, leaving an odd heaviness. Jack stirred beside her, turned over and reached out for her, drawing her into his embrace. He muttered something she couldn't understand.

She didn't sleep again. She watched the darkness fade into dawn, heard the chorus of birds greet the new morning. The sun filled the room with golden light, filtering through the thin curtains that fluttered in front of the open windows. She allowed the new light to fill her mind, to chase away the feeling of doom. After all, it had only been a dream.

Jack took her on a tour of the area that day—a glorious sunny day. They explored Roman ruins and ancient villages with cobblestone streets, and visited a farmers' market overflowing with spring produce—asparagus, cherries, strawberries, all kinds of lettuces. She loved the displays of rustic country breads, fresh herbs and cheeses.

They had lunch on a restaurant terrace in the shade of enormous trees, feasting on thick slices of pâté, crusty bread, olives and gherkins and cheese, skipping a main course that would surely have put her in a food-induced stupor for the rest of the afternoon.

"This place is a food-lovers' paradise. I think I could live here," Christina said with a longing sigh as they strolled back to the car Jack had hired.

"I try to bring the kids here at least once a year," Jack said as he fished the keys from his pocket. "I'd like them to keep in touch with their family roots and history. You think you could settle for a visit once a year?"

He was including her in his future. Next year, and the next. She smiled. "I think I could, probably," she said lightly.

He opened the door for her and she slipped into the passenger seat.

"Nana would certainly be happy to have you here again," he said, sliding in behind the wheel. "She's been singing your praises to me."

The palms of her hands were suddenly damp. She knew what else was being said. Nicole had told her last night, whispering the words with a touch of glee: "Everybody thinks Dad should marry you! It's so cool!"

*   *   *

After dinner that night, they went on a stroll through the garden, sweet with the fragrance of jasmine and roses. A large, full moon hung over the placid Mediterranean and the breeze was cool on her skin.

At the far end of the garden, stone steps descended to the beach and they carefully made their way down. The water glimmered seductively. He pulled her beside him to sit in the sand, still warm from the day's sun. Putting his arms around her, he kissed her.

"I've been wanting to do this for hours," he murmured against her lips. She put her arms around his neck and kissed him back, and he pressed her close against him.

How wonderful it was to feel her body come alive, to feel her heart sing with desire.

"Christina?"

"Mmm . . . yes."

"You know I love you?"

"Yes," she whispered back.

"You know what I want more than anything in life?"

"Mmm . . . what?"

"I want us to be together always. I want you to be my wife. Will you please marry me?"

She stiffened. It happened automatically, instinctively, and his answering reaction of withdrawal was almost instant. He sat back from her, staring at her in the pale moonlight.

"Good God, Christina," he said huskily, "you'd think I'd made you an indecent proposal."

"I'm sorry." Her heart was pumping hard, the blood throbbing in her head. "I . . . I wasn't expecting it."

He hadn't talked about marriage for months. She'd hoped he'd settled into the comfortable, easy relationship they had together and found it enough, as she did.

"Christina, all I want is for you to be my wife. For us to belong together."

"Why do we have to be married for that?" She hugged herself as if she were cold. Only it wasn't cold.

He searched her face. "Maybe it sounds terribly selfish, but I want to be number one in your life. I want to feel that you are committed to me, to our relationship."

She swallowed. "I am committed to you. You know that."

His face worked. "Do I? I'm not always so sure, Christina." His voice was bleak.

She swallowed. "Why not? What do you mean?"

"I'm often aware of an emotional reserve in you, a distance you're keeping. I wonder sometimes if you really love me."

She flinched at the pain in his voice. "I do love you," she said huskily.

"Then why are you holding back? There's always this distance. As if you're prepared to run off at any moment."

"Run off?"

"Away from me."

She was shaking her head. "I...I don't want to run away from you, Jack. I don't know why you think that."

"I hoped it would get better with time, but it's not." His hands were balled into fists. She saw the tension in the rigid line of his shoulders.

"I feel as if you're expecting me to do something wrong at any moment," he went on, his voice low with frustration. "The moment I mention marriage, you freeze up on me."

"Well, I've never been crazy about being married," she said tightly, her hands grasping uselessly at the sand.

"You weren't crazy about *being married to Peter*!" He leaped to his feet, towering over her, his posture unbending. "I resent your assuming I'll do what your husband did! Dammit, Christina! How dare you allow that man to influence your life still? How dare you think I'll treat you the same way?" He raked his hands through his hair. "I don't understand you," he admitted. "You are a smart, intelligent woman. How can you think this way?"

Christina sat frozen in the sand, the words washing over her, drowning her. She couldn't breathe, couldn't think.

He stood in front of her, looming tall in the dark, his bulk blocking out the moon. "What do you want me to do?" he demanded. "Why in hell are you so distrustful of me? What have I ever done to deserve that?"

She swallowed. Her tongue wouldn't move.

"What have I ever done to deserve that, Christina?" he repeated. "Tell me!"

She shook her head. "Nothing," she whispered. It was true.

"Then why?"

"I don't know." She began to shake. "Stop shouting at me!" she managed, scrambling to her feet. "I can't help feeling the way I do!" Tears of anguish filled her eyes. "I'm sorry!" She turned and ran, or tried to run. The shifting sand made her stumble. Losing her balance, she fell to her knees, feeling like an idiot. Before Jack could help her, she'd struggled to her feet and made her way back to the house more slowly, staying well ahead of him.

Family members were everywhere in the house and on the terrace, talking, laughing. There was no place to go but her bedroom, which Jack was sharing with her in favor of the small one they'd given him next door for propriety's sake.

She was sitting on the side of the bed, taking in gulps of air, when he came in a few moments later, offering her a glass of wine.

"You can't run away from this, Christina," he said, his voice flat. "We have to talk."

Saying nothing, she sipped the wine, not looking at him.

He paced the room, head bent, hands in his pockets. "I've tried to understand you," he said, voice low, a voice straining with control. "I've tried to be patient, to give you time to get used to me—to us, to what we are together and what it means to me. What *you* mean to me." He paused. Then he turned slowly to face her. "I love you. I want you to be my wife. I don't want an affair with us living in two different places. I want to be with you every day—go to bed with you, wake up with you. What the hell is wrong with that, Christina?"

She swallowed miserably. "Nothing." She wished she knew what to say. It all sounded so wonderful, so idyllic, the way she had always wanted it. Being together with Jack for the rest of her life, how could she not want it? Of course she wanted it. She wanted it more than anything, yet the thought of marriage nearly choked her, made her heart go wild with uncontrollable fear. She could hardly breathe. She couldn't do it.

"Then why won't you marry me?"

"I'm scared," she whispered.

"Scared of what?"

"Lots of things. Your wife . . . she was so wonderful, and I'm not. I'm afraid of failing you, of not being good enough, of your leaving me." Oh, God, why had she said that? She had not known she would say that; the words had come out by themselves. She sounded so pathetic, so insecure. This person speaking was the old, anxiety-ridden self she'd thought had been cured.

But it hadn't been cured, and the dream she'd had should have warned her.

His jaw was like iron. "You're driving me crazy with this stuff! Why won't you be good enough? Because that husband of yours thought you weren't? The man was a heap of insecurities, projecting them onto you. I am *not* your ex-husband, Christina!" Anger radiated from him.

She sat on the edge of the bed like a statue, gazing into her glass, feeling the tension crackling in the air, touching her skin. She held her breath.

"If you don't trust me now, Christina, then I don't think you ever will." The bitterness in his voice filled the room. "I love you, but I can't make you trust me. I don't know what else I have to do to make you believe me. And if there's no trust, there's not much point in going on. I don't want an endless affair."

Her mouth went dry. "What are you saying?" The words were barely a whisper and terror squeezed her chest.

"I'm saying that I don't want to go on this way." He shoved his balled hands into his pockets. "I want you for my wife, to love and cherish and grow old with." Pain twisted his face. "If I can't make you feel safe with me, then this relationship isn't working and there's no point in continuing it."

CHAPTER TWELVE

HER chest felt as if somebody had been throwing rocks at it. She couldn't breathe, couldn't talk. Panic gripped her.

It was over, their relationship finished.

"Jack, please," she whispered. "Please, don't do this."

"I'm sorry." His face worked as if he wanted to say something more, but couldn't get the words out. Grief made his face look old. He turned abruptly and strode out of the room.

Outside, a songbird warbled in the evening silence, a lovely, ethereal sound, but it did nothing to stir her heart. Her heart felt like stone; her mouth tasted like ashes. But when she looked in the mirror in her room, she saw her face wet with tears.

She didn't know how long she sat on the edge of the bed, minutes, hours, fighting off the anguish, failing. Slowly the misery seeped into every bone and muscle, but she refused to cry. There was no time for crying now. Maybe later, when she was far away from here.

She'd have to leave. She couldn't stay here any longer. Tomorrow morning, first thing, she would call a taxi. She would go back home, accept the job in South Carolina and start over.

In a feverish haste, her hands trembling, she opened the closet to get her suitcase. A knock on the door startled her. "Yes?" Her voice squeaked oddly and she

179

moved to the door and opened it, her legs feeling wooden.

It was Nicole, smiling. "Remember I told you about the dog we had when I was little?" she asked. "The one that died a couple of years ago?"

"Yes, I do." Christina willed herself to sound normal, to look normal.

"I found a picture of her when she was a puppy," Nicole went on. "Nana had it in her album. Look." She handed Christina the picture in her hand. "She was sitting in my mom's lap." She frowned. "It's not a very good picture of my mom, though."

Christina took the photograph and looked at it, at the woman holding the puppy in her lap. Her heart turned over with shock.

Oh, my God, she thought silently, oh, my God.

CHAPTER THIRTEEN

CHRISTINA looked at the picture, knowing she had to say something to Nicole, something about the puppy, but all she could focus on was the woman's face. Sara's face.

She had seen that face before, on a photo in Nicole's bedroom, a beautiful face in profile.

This was not a profile picture, but it displayed the same dark, curly hair and large brown eyes. It also showed the right side of her face.

Christina's heart contracted. The right side of Sara's face was contorted, masklike, as if it had been ripped apart and put together wrong.

"Isn't she cute?" said Nicole.

Christina swallowed a laugh of hysteria. Cute. The dog, of course. She nodded, trying to find her voice. "Yes, she's very cute, and so little." She moved to the bed and sat down, afraid her legs would give out. Memories came back—Jack telling her Sara had been in a bad accident as a girl; the woman at the party saying something about Jack falling in love with Sara, something about it being hard in the beginning. Because of Sara's face, she'd meant. She hadn't understood it then, not knowing.

Nicole sat down next to her. "She grew really fast, but I remember when she was small like that. She was so adorable, you know." Nicole paused for a moment, her gaze on the snapshot in her hand. "I don't remember my mom looking like that, you know," she said softly. "I mean, she always did, but it was just the way

she was and I never thought about it when I was little."
She bit her lip. "I guess I was just used to it."

Christina swallowed painfully, knowing she had to say
something, anything. "Your mom was very special, your
dad told me. You must have loved her a lot." The words
came of their own accord, borne from an unknown place
of strength inside her.

"Oh, yes, I did. Sometimes other kids would tease me
and say my mother was ugly, and I would get so mad!
And now, when I look at pictures like this, I can see
why they thought so, but to me she was never ugly."

Christina's heart contracted and a lump formed in her
throat.

"Because she was your mother, and you loved her."

"Yeah." Nicole sighed. "Sometimes I feel guilty, you
know, when I look at myself and I think I'm not very
pretty because my nose is funny or I wish I had blond
hair or I wish I looked like somebody else, like some
movie star, and then I think of my mother and I feel
kind of guilty."

"Everybody feels like that at your age, Nicole." Again
the words came from a secret source of strength. "It's
part of growing up, comparing yourself with other kids
and thinking you don't measure up. You'll get over it
as you grow older and get a better idea of who you are."

Listen to what you're saying! a small voice said in her
head. *Do you hear yourself*?

"And you really are very pretty, even if you don't think
so yourself."

Nicole sighed. "Dad says it's fine to be pretty, but
that other things are much more important, you know,
like the kind of person you are."

"That's true."

"That's why he loved my mom, because of the kind
of person she was." Nicole glanced up, smiling now.

"And that's why he loves you. Because you're a good person." She grinned. "But you're pretty, too."

Christina didn't know whether to laugh or cry. "Thank you," she said. She handed back the picture. "Sometimes I'm not at all sure I'm a good person." She didn't feel like a very good one now. She felt small and petty.

"Oh, but you are! Everybody thinks so. You're so nice to Nana and that's a good sign. A lot of people don't want to bother with very old people, but you do. You spent hours in the kitchen making her a special dessert because the cook didn't know how to do it, and you talk to her all the time and make her laugh."

"She makes me laugh, too. She's a great old lady."

"Well, I think you're great, too." Nicole threw her arms around Christina and hugged her. She had never done that before, and as if embarrassed by her own impulsiveness, she jumped to her feet and almost ran from the room, tossing a hasty good-night over her shoulder.

Christina sat on the edge of the bed, staring at the photo that must have slipped from Nicole's fingers and dropped to the floor.

Everything was confused in her mind, everything turned upside down. She was looking at the sainted Sara, the woman everyone adored and admired, the woman Jack had loved truly and deeply for fourteen years. Sara hadn't been glamorous and beautiful the way she had always imagined her. The wife Jack had loved had been a woman with half her face cruelly disfigured.

The face blurred in front of her and her eyes swam with tears. "Oh, Jack," she whispered, "I'm so sorry, so sorry. Why did I ever doubt you?"

Because you didn't trust yourself, the little voice answered inside her head. *You didn't think you were good enough*.

He had loved his wife in spite of her ravaged face. Had married her with it. He'd loved her for what she was, not because she was a piece of property he could show off to the world, to enhance his own image. He wasn't like Peter, would never be Peter. Peter had always worried about other people's opinions of him, about what people would think and say about what he did. She remembered Jack's stories about himself as a boy, about how he had always gone his own way, not caring about fitting in or doing what was proper. He knew what he wanted, who he was. He didn't have to prove anything to anybody. Peter was always trying to prove himself, always worried about his image.

How could she have been so blind? Fear had blinded her. Fear was going to cause her to lose what she wanted most in the world—Jack's love.

Fear and insecurity—so insidious—had permeated all her feelings and thoughts, ravaging her ability to see the truth. And it had taken Sara to make her see the light.

Jack loved her. He wanted her and he didn't need her to be gorgeous. He didn't need her to show her off to anybody. He didn't need her to be any different than the person she was.

She hadn't trusted Jack because she hadn't trusted herself, her own value as a woman.

She stared at the photo, at the warm brown eyes that looked back at her, across time, across space. Eyes that smiled, reassured.

He loves you now. Love him back. He needs you. She could hear the words being spoken somewhere in her mind. Lifting her head, she saw the darkness outside her window. It was night. She was alone in this room, communing with a dead woman. A woman she'd perceived as a threat. A woman who had now offered her a gift of love.

It was very late, she realized. In the small room next door was Jack. Alone, too. Was he asleep? Lying awake?

She had treated him abominably. He was a good man, a wonderful man, and he had offered her his heart and soul and she had rejected him. Oh, God, it was so awful.

She had to find him and tell him she loved him, wanted to marry him and never feel doubt again. She swallowed at the constriction in her throat, felt painful tears slide down her face. She moved as if in a trance, out of the room. Jack's bedroom door was closed. She knocked, but no answer came. She opened the door quietly. The room was in darkness.

"Jack?" she whispered.

No answer. She advanced into the room, her eyes adjusting to the dark. He was there, lying on top of the bed covers, fully dressed.

"Jack?" she said a little louder.

"Christina?" He sat up and turned on the bedside lamp.

"Yes." She blinked against the sudden light, taking a step back from the bed. "Did I wake you?"

"No. Why are you here?" His tone was even, giving nothing away.

She swallowed. "Can we talk, please?" Her voice trembled. She closed the door behind her and leaned against it for support.

"I'm not sure what else there is to say."

She fought against the tears and the fear that threatened to engulf her. "You said I didn't trust you. That you couldn't make me feel safe with you."

"Yes."

"The real truth is that I didn't trust myself, that secretly I didn't think I was worth loving." She dragged in a deep breath. "I feel so awful, because you've done everything possible to show me differently and...and..." Her voice faltered and tears began to run down her cheeks. She was grateful for the support of the door at her back. "I'm so sorry," she whispered and then her throat closed and she couldn't talk anymore, couldn't say all the things she wanted him to know, to understand. She began to cry with deep, aching sobs.

He jumped to his feet, enfolded her in his arms. "Christina, please, don't cry, don't cry."

"I'm so sorry," she wept. "I'm so sorry for everything. For not trusting you, for not trusting myself, for being blind and stupid."

"That's a lot," he said dryly.

"There's more," she said miserably. "I'm so messed up, but will you marry me anyway?"

He didn't say anything, but she felt an odd trembling in his body. And then she realised he was laughing. *Laughing!*

"This isn't funny!" she sobbed. "Don't laugh!"

"Oh, sweetheart, it feels so good to laugh! And yes, I'll marry you—blind, stupid and messed up. As long as you really want me."

"I really, really want you," she said huskily, relief flooding her. "With all my heart and all my soul," she added theatrically. "We can get married tomorrow if you want."

He smiled, a happy light in his eyes. "How about today? It's after midnight."

"Today will be fine." Her heart began to glow. She felt alive and whole as never before.

He reached for something on the dresser behind her. "Look what I've got for you. Give me your left hand."

With breathless anticipation, she watched as he slipped a ring on her finger—an exquisite antique ring with a huge star sapphire encircled by round diamonds alongside a scalloped border accented with tiny diamonds. The breath caught in her throat. It was gorgeous, ornamental and no doubt worth a fortune. It weighed half a ton. It was a museum piece.

He studied her face, humor in his eyes. "You like it?"

"It's beautiful," she said truthfully. Beautiful for a museum piece. She wondered if she would ever be able to wear the thing anywhere without needing a wrist support. Not to speak of a bodyguard to protect her. "You bought this for me?" she asked, hoping she didn't sound too incredulous.

Laughter danced in his eyes. "Good grief, no. Nana gave it to me to give to you. She said she'd disown me if I didn't marry you."

She felt the laughter bubble up inside her. "So that's why you want me to marry you."

"You bet." He pressed her hard against him, holding her as if he'd never let go. "It's just for the money."

MILLS & BOON®

Next Month's Romances

♡

Each month you can choose from a wide variety of romance novels from Mills & Boon. Below are the new titles to look out for next month from the Presents and Enchanted series.

Presents™

JACK'S BABY	Emma Darcy
A MARRYING MAN?	Lindsay Armstrong
ULTIMATE TEMPTATION	Sara Craven
THE PRICE OF A WIFE	Helen Brooks
GETTING EVEN	Sharon Kendrick
TEMPTING LUCAS	Catherine Spencer
MAN TROUBLE!	Natalie Fox
A FORGOTTEN MAGIC	Kathleen O'Brien

Enchanted™

HUSBANDS ON HORSEBACK	
	Margaret Way & Diana Palmer
MACBRIDE'S DAUGHTER	Patricia Wilson
MARRYING THE BOSS!	Leigh Michaels
THE DADDY PROJECT	Suzanne Carey
BEHAVING BADLY!	Emma Richmond
A DOUBLE WEDDING	Patricia Knoll
TAKEOVER ENGAGEMENT	Elizabeth Duke
HUSBAND-TO-BE	Linda Miles

Available from WH Smith, John Menzies, Volume One, Forbuoys, Martins, Woolworths, Tesco, Asda, Safeway and other paperback stockists.

MILLS & BOON

Weddings ❖ Glamour ❖ Family ❖ Heartbreak

Weddings By DeWilde

Since the turn of the century, the elegant and fashionable
DeWilde stores have helped brides around the world
realise the fantasy of their 'special day'.

*For weddings, romance and glamour,
enter the world of*

Weddings By DeWilde

**—a fantastic line up of 12 new stories from popular
Mills & Boon authors**

MARCH 1997

Bk. 11 ROMANCING THE STONES - Janis Flores
Bk. 12 I DO, AGAIN - Jasmine Cresswell

'Happy' Greetings!

Would you like to win a year's supply of Mills & Boon® books? Well you can and they're free! Simply complete the competition below and send it to us by 31st August 1997. The first five correct entries picked after the closing date will each win a year's subscription to the Mills & Boon series of their choice. What could be easier?

ACSPPMTHYHARSI

—————— —————————

TPHEEYPSARA

————— ——————

RAHIHPYBDYTAP

—————— ————————

NHMYRTSPAAPNERUY

————— —————— ————————

DYVLTEPYAANINSEPAH

————— —————— ————————

YAYPNAHPEREW

————— ——————

DMHPYAHRYOSETPA

—————— —————————

VRHYPNARSAEYNPIA

—————— —————————

Please turn over for details of how to enter ☞

How to enter...

There are eight jumbled up greetings overleaf, most of which you will probably hear at some point throughout the year. Each of the greetings is a 'happy' one, i.e. the word 'happy' is somewhere within it. All you have to do is identify each greeting and write your answers in the spaces provided. Good luck!

When you have unravelled each greeting don't forget to fill in your name and address in the space provided and tick the Mills & Boon® series you would like to receive if you are a winner. Then simply pop this page into an envelope (you don't even need a stamp) and post it today. Hurry—competition ends 31st August 1997.

Mills & Boon 'Happy' Greetings Competition
FREEPOST, Croydon, Surrey, CR9 3WZ

Please tick the series you would like to receive if you are a winner

Presents™ ❏   Enchanted™ ❏   Medical Romance™ ❏
Historical Romance™ ❏   Temptation® ❏

Are you a Reader Service Subscriber?   Yes ❏   No ❏

Ms/Mrs/Miss/Mr _____

(BLOCK CAPS PLEASE)

Address _____

_____

_____ Postcode _____

(I am over 18 years of age)

One application per household. Competition open to residents of the UK and Ireland only.
You may be mailed with other offers from other reputable companies as a result of this application. If you would prefer not to receive such offers, please tick box. ❏

mps
MAILING
PREFERENCE
SERVICE

C7B